THE BEYOND

THE *Dan* DIARIES

d. d. marx

The Dan Diaries

Copyright © 2018 D. D. Marx

Contributors: Cover Illustration: Michael Fitzpatrick; Graphic Design by Morpheus Blak for Critical Mass Communications; Content Editor: Caroline Tolley; Copy Editor: Tim Jacobs Writing Consultants

ISBN: 978-0-9972481-7-3 paperback

Printed in the United States of America

To order, go to:
www.ddmarx.com

DEDICATION

The Dan Diaries is dedicated to my Austin family, the Grey's, for hosting me and treating me as one of their own during my writing process. Also, to my friends at 'The Workplace' in Dripping Spring, Texas for providing an inspiring space and environment to write, enhancing my creativity. Last but certainly not least, to my partner in crime and co-pilot Patty for literally being with me from the first word of the series to the very last! I couldn't have done it without any of you guys. Much love! xo

THE DAN DIARIES

CHAPTER ONE

"*HAAAAAANK,*" I scream when an oncoming driver, crosses over the median, and I feel an abrupt and jarring impact. My car spins around. I hear the sound of broken glass, metal scraping metal, and screeching of tires. Everything goes black.

I don't feel any pain; just a warmish sensation running through my body. My unfamiliar surroundings, appear tranquil and serene when I hear a voice whisper, "Welcome, Daniel."

"Who are *you?*" I ask, still waiting to snap out of it. That's when I notice that I'm hovering over my own physical body, still pinned in the driver's seat of my cherry red Chevy Cavalier.

"I'm your assigned angel, Gabriel." My mind racing while he awaits my response.

Angel? What? Did I DIE? How is this possible? I'm in the prime of my life. I'm on the phone making Easter brunch plans and now what? It's all over? Surely, this is a mistake. Is HE testing me? Teaching me a valuable lesson to be more attentive? To not take anything for granted? I can't just be gone, right? I'm sure the doctors will revive me, and I'll tell everyone what a crazy experience this is.

My eyes dart back down to see the paramedics using the jaws of life to remove me from the car. They administer CPR as they race me to the ambulance. A police officer picks up my phone and calls Hank, well — Olivia Henry, my best friend. I was on the phone with her when the accident happened. He describes the terrible accident and instructs her to call my parents and meet us at the hospital.

Now I can see Hank. What a *strange* feeling. I can see anything and everything I concentrate my mind on. I begin yelling,

HANK, HANK, *I'm right here; it's okay, it's okay. I can see you.*

I see her sobbing while speeding to the hospital. I turn back to Gabriel.

"Please tell me they revive me."

I want to reach out to touch her, to reassure her that everything is going to be okay.

"I'm afraid not."

"*What?* No, No. This can't happen. My family is going to be devastated." I pace back and forth, not paying any attention to my surroundings.

"Yes, you're right. They'll experience tremendous loss from losing you, but their faith will get them through the difficult times ahead."

"I don't mean any disrespect, but aren't there other people *HE* can take? Like terrorists, murderers, drug dealers . . . to rattle off a few. I mean, I'm sure this place . . . whatever this is . . . is *spectacular*." I gesture around with my hands waving. "I never dreamt I'd arrive before a ripe old age."

"I understand. *HE* says this happens with the all younger ones, especially when they're taken in a tragedy like this. There are always so many questions. You need clarity, which is why *HE* gives you a transition period. "

"How long is the transition period?"

"It varies with each soul, but yours is a week — in human terms. It gives you time to process your feelings as your family lays you to rest."

2

"How come I'm so heartbroken? Shouldn't I feel euphoric?" I glance down at the emergency room waiting area as my parents arrive.

"You'll keep all of your physical emotions during this transition process. Once you cross over, there is no more doubt, pain or suffering. The primary emotion is exuberance. You'll experience an overabundance of everything, especially love and happiness."

"Why can't I choose to go back if I haven't officially crossed over? Shouldn't it still be my own free will?"

"You see, Daniel, the accident was too devastating. The other driver swerved to avoid a car that crossed into his lane. You don't remember anything, but the impact severed your spine. You'd be confined to a wheelchair and would lose your vivacious spirit. Your family and friends would suffer even more, witnessing you die on the inside. It is *HE* who determines when each soul transitions. It was your time. *HE* must have important work for you. You'll find out when you meet *HIM*."

"When will I get to meet *HIM*?"

"Shortly. I'll explain more when you're ready. For now, I'll be over in my office. Feel free to come in whenever you're ready or have any questions. Until then, take the time to get comfortable with being gone."

My attention turns back to the hospital waiting room where the doctor is approaching my family and Hank to deliver the news. *This is horrendous. I can't bear to think of the pain they're experiencing right now.*

\#

To distract myself, I decide to take a brief tour to investigate my environment. So far, it feels as if I'm in the lowest level of a video game. A parallel dimension. When you first play, you need to get your bearings before you can advance to the next room. The best way to describe where I'm at right now is a dentist office waiting room, only the waiting room is enormous. Multiply the size of the waiting room by inifinity. It's lit with overhead fluorescent lighting. Furnishings are limited to beige sectional sofas and recliners. The long hallway in front of me is covered in monochromatic shades of blue and gray paint. Posters cover the walls with sayings.

If you want to make God laugh, tell HIM your plans.

I'm in stitches reading that one. *Nice touch. At least I know You do have a good sense of humor.*

At the end of the hall, there is a giant door with a sign displayed — *The Other Side.* I can't see any stairs, elevator, or doors, but there is elevator-like music playing. *Jazz.* This space is pleasant but not somewhere you'd want to stay for long. It smells fresh, like a crisp spring day after a cold winter. The temperature is perfect, not too hot and not too cold. There isn't anyone else around me. I can only see Gabriel off in the distance. I'm not hungry, thirsty or tired. I don't have a sense of time; it's almost as if I'm paused. Standing still. The air is thick, almost fog-like, casting a slight veil over everything. When I concentrate hard, visions of the physical world become crystal clear. I'm there in the moment, only no one can see or hear me, like a time warp. *Trippy.*

The most dominant emotion I'm feeling now is determination. I must find a way to communicate with everyone. I may be gone, but I want them to feel my presence. *But how can I do that? There must be a way. I mean, I'm ripped away without any warning. Just a regular, ordinary day. I still can't believe this.* I miss them so much already, only I know I have something amazing awaiting me on the other side of *that* door. They are left in complete agony, suffering from unimaginable grief and despair. It's a tough pill to swallow, to leave my friends and family like this. I want nothing more than to comfort them and tell them it's going to be okay. We'll all be together again someday. In the meantime, I'll watch over them for every moment of each day.

The biggest challenge on earth is now crystal clear. You spend your whole life trying to imagine *if* and *what* awaits you when you die. No one knows. There isn't any proof. You must rely on your own internal beliefs. Your interpretation of faith, hope and love. There are never any guarantees. The world fills you with constant doubt. You experience challenging times. I don't want my death to be a waste. I want to cause disruption and help to unveil the mystery of the other side. Prove that we're really still here. I want to be the one to leave more answers than questions. To be the proof they are seeking. I mean, not be *HIM*, of course, that isn't possible, but I want the ability to leave a trail of breadcrumbs. Little details that help to guide and reassure them that I'm not *gone*, gone. I'm still here, just invisible. I need to provide some level of comfort to the amazing people who love me endlessly that I'm being forced to leave behind — like Hank. She'll never recover from this. Her name was the last word out of my mouth. She'll never let that go. She'll replay it in her head *over* and over.

#

Olivia Henry is my best friend. Everyone calls her Liv. I call her Hank — short for Henry. That's my schtick. I give everyone nicknames because nicknames are fun and endearing. They describe, in one intimate word, the unspoken bond connecting our lives. Only those closest to you are lucky enough to use nicknames and share inside jokes. It's a sacred space designed for only those people you consider the most special.

I've known Hank since the ripe age of fourteen. The very first day of high school. I remember it vividly. I can't explain what it is about her. It's like our souls always knew each other. The connection was instant. I'm drawn to her. She feels like home in an environment that's unpredictable, fragile and vulnerable. There isn't any romantic vibe between us, but I love her more than any "girlfriend." She's a cross between my sister and my best buddy. She can hang. She isn't high maintenance. She doesn't nag and isn't ever needy. There's no drama with her. We can be ourselves in any moment and not worry about being judged or unloved. That's why she's the one I like spending time with the most. We laugh so hard together. We have the exact same sense of humor. I can't explain it. No one else gets my humor like her. It's unspoken. A simple look can send us into a spiral.

We spend summers at my lake house and attend countless concerts together. My parents are huge music fans, so it must be hereditary. I taught Hank everything she knows about music. Our taste spans the full spectrum of music genres. We love rock and roll, country, and everything in between. One of our favorites is John Mellencamp. His songs are relatable, and the lyrics describe our lives in brief moments, small town kids with big time dreams.

Just as the thought crosses my mind, I see her. She's in her bedroom, going through boxes of memorabilia. We have this random tradition where we send each other postcards from interesting destinations when we're not together. *Aww, I never thought she would save this stuff.* She's reading the postcard from my first day in college and *whoa*, it refers to John Mellencamp. *Wow, now that is crazy.*

> *Hank,*
> *Can't wait to see you at Homecoming in a few weeks.*
> *Have you heard Mellencamp's new song "If I Die Sudden"?*
> *Miss you! XO Danny*

"Oh my God. Danny, can you hear me? Where are you? I miss you so much it's unbearable. You must find a way to let me know you're okay. If you can hear me, send me a Mellencamp song. No, send me 'Small Town,'" Hank begs.

"HANK . . . yes, *yes*, it's me, I can hear you. I can see you. I'm *RIGHT HERE*," I shout, overcome with emotion, agonizing over how sad she is. I want to reach out and hug her. Comfort her. Talk to her. Tell her that I love her one last time. Surely, she knows how much, right? We didn't say it often, but it was obvious. There is no friend I love more.

I look up and see Gabriel. He's intervening because he can see that I'm in distress.

"How are you doing?"

"It's Hank; she's talking to me and . . . I just want to reach out to comfort her. Tell her I'm here. I'll always be here. This feels impossible."

"I know, Daniel. Things will start to make sense soon. I promise. Is there anything I can do? Can I answer any questions for you?" I finally remember who he really is. He is an *Angel* after all. I haven't even taken a moment to let that sink in. I should study and observe him to gain some insight as to where I'm going.

Being raised Catholic, you're taught all about Angels. You're told that we each have a Guardian Angel who watches over us. They're souls that pass before us and come back to protect us from harm. Some we know and some we don't, but we all have them. If I were to describe one, based on memory, I would characterize an Angel as being a bright, white but translucent apparition with wings. They're elusive but always around you. They go undetected. Gabriel is *nothing* like this. Not to be sacrilegious, but he looks like any other guy. I mean, he looks like my last *Uber driver. Nothing* about him screams, *I'm one of the chosen ones,* which is ironic. *Huh. Interesting.* He's young-ish. I'd say early twenties, healthy build, good head of thick brown hair. He's about six feet tall, clean shaven and wearing non-descript clothes — a pair of blue jeans and a gray, cotton baseball t-shirt with navy sleeves. Something you'd get at Old Navy.

"Ummm, did you die in that?" I ask.

"*Excuse me?*"

"Oh, sorry, sorry! I'm not trying to be a jerk. I've been so preoccupied with my friends' and family's situation that I haven't taken one second to *really* look at you. Now that I have, I guess my question is — where did you get your clothes? Did you die in those?"

"Ummm, no, I definitely *understood* the question. I don't know why you're asking it."

"I know it seems random, but I am just wondering what it's like on the other side of that door? Are there stores over there or am I going to spend eternity in these jeans, flannel, Cubs hat, and white Chuck Taylor high-tops?" I can tell I've offended him. "Sorry, I really don't want to get off on the wrong foot here."

"*HE* gave me a heads up on you. I didn't know it would start *this* early."

"What do you mean?"

"When I was assigned your case, I was given this note card describing you."

He hands it to me to read.

Name: Daniel Mark Sullivan

Features: 5'11; Medium Build; Sandy Brown Hair; Blue Eyes; Dimples for days

"Ha," I laugh, reading it.

"I presume that laugh is in response to the *dimples for days* description. I thought maybe He should assign you a female." I continue reading.

Characteristics: thoughtful; kind; charismatic; mischievous; generous; charming; endearing

Best known for: being a great hugger; having a distinctive, striking, and contagious laugh;and being a loving son, brother, and forever friend.

Special notes: extremely funny (sophisticated sense of humor) and very handsome.

9

"So yeah, when I got the debrief, *HE* told me you are a bit of a comedian — self-deprecating and extremely sarcastic. And *here* it is. You clearly didn't waste any time displaying it. You're not even *in* yet."

"*Oh no*, am I at risk of not getting *in?*" I say with concern.

"*Nah.* I'm messing with you, man. You're totally *in.* This is my *first* official Angel gig. I didn't know what to expect. I thought I'd at least start off very "angelic-like." You know, stoic and serious, almost uptight."

"That's odd that *HE* would assign you to me then. I'm nothing like that."

"I can see that," he says. "So, we should start over."

"Okay."

"What's up . . . *my maaan.* My name isn't Gabriel either. I went with it to seem like I had some street cred. My real name's Jake Ryan." He reaches out to give me a huge bro-hug. "Pleased to make your acquaintance."

"*Jake Ryan?* Like the dude from *Sixteen Candles?*" I chuckle.

"Yep. My parents are huge eighties buffs."

"Now that's funny," I respond, embracing him. "I mean, I've been racking my brain trying to figure out how to get back. I wasn't sure if I'd be stuck with you — forever. No offense, but you didn't come across as someone I could spend eternity with."

"Totally get it, bro. Zero offense taken. Yeah, so anyway, this place is *totally* cool. It's like the physical world, only all the best parts. For example, the weather. It's never cloudy, gloomy, cold, rainy. It's bright, sunny, and 82° all the time. The colors are infinitely more vibrant: greens, blues, and yellows that are indescribable. We have cars, stores, coffee, beer.

You know, all the essentials and no money required. There's enough of everything for anyone who wants it."

"*Beer?*" I recline in one of the chairs, making myself comfortable. My attempt at loosening up. Then, out of nowhere, a giant tray of loaded nachos, buffalo wings, pepperoni pizza, and a pitcher of beer appears in front of me.

"*Whoa.* What just happened?"

"The more settled in you feel, the more things will happen. Like I said, an abundance of all your favorite things. Oh and no hangovers . . . which, if I'm being honest, is one of my favorite things so far."

"So, you never feel things like anger, sadness, loneliness or despair here? You can't get sick or hurt?" I dig into the snacks and pour myself an ice-cold beer.

"Nope. It's perfection on the grandest scale. We're going to be *best* friends over there." He points at the door.

"Well, if they have beer, then I guess we can be friends," I reply with a mouth full of nachos, giving him a smirk.

"It really is un-believe-able. I truly can't describe it in words. Remarkable. Magnificent. Spectacular. Beyond comprehension."

"What's *HE* like?"

"The hippest, coolest dude you could ever hope to know: generous, humble, charismatic, thoughtful, funny, and *super* smart. The one negative is sometimes *HE* comes off as a 'know-it-all,' which can get fairly annoying," he says, being all serious. "*Ahhhh,* I'm messing with you again, man. *HE's* everything you've heard about *HIM*, very down to earth."

"*Clever.* I see what you did there. Is *HE* intimidating?"

"*Nah. HE* created you. *HE* knows you better than you know yourself. *HE* knows exactly what you're going to say or do before you do it. Kind of like the whole Santa Claus thing." He laughs. "You can be exactly who you are. *HE* wouldn't expect anything less. In fact, *HE* knew we'd get along; that's why *HE* sent me."

"So, what's your story?"

"I'm from a small town near Fort Thomas, Kentucky. I died six weeks ago. Same deal. Car accident. Hence, the reason I'm assigned to you. We have similar stories."

"How are you adjusting?"

"I'm not going to lie; it's been rough. It's hard to see everyone you love destroyed and inconsolable. I'm told my new job will help with this feeling. I haven't found out what it is yet. *HE* said we'd start together."

"We have to work?"

"Technically, no. This is our designated higher purpose."

"You've done a great job of distracting me for the moment, but I'm still in major distress over leaving everyone behind."

"It's completely natural. Once you settle in, you'll find ways to communicate. You'll learn that in your first meeting with *HIM*."

"Can you stay here with me while I suffer through the rest of this?" I ask.

"Of course. That's why I'm here."

"Can you see her, too?" I ask, concentrating on bringing Hank into focus.

"Who? *Hank*? Yeah. Dude, she's hot. How did you not tap that?" he says, flinching in case I deck him.

"Don't push your luck," I say with a glare.

CHAPTER TWO

The funeral is today, so Jake is giving me space. So many people show up from all parts of my life — grade school, high school, college. All my extended family is here. My immediate family is holding up much better than expected. We are such a strong family; I shouldn't be surprised. Hank is the biggest basket case, which I anticipated. She is not equipped for this. She has such a warm, tender, and loving heart. The biggest of anyone I know. She is fun loving, a true-blue love of life. She sees everything as the glass half full. She is the cheerleader in everyone else's life. She has this naivety about her, always seeing the bright side.

Nothing prepares you for a tragedy like this, especially not for someone so close to you. She's shattered. She has Red, our other best friend from high school. Red — well, Susan Graham. Of course, I gave her the nickname, Red. She has the longest, beautiful auburn hair. We call ourselves the three musketeers, but deep-down Red knows Hank and I have an unspoken connection. No one can penetrate it, not even her. She's not threatened by it. She knows her place. She and Hank have their own feminine connection, so it works. Right now, I'm most grateful for Red, Hank's older sister, Jane, and her cousin Garrett. They will be the foundation Hank needs to get through this ordeal. They will be the new musketeers. Jane is two years older than Hank, but they've always been close. Garrett Stanford is Hank's first cousin.

They've never lived in the same city, but they spent all their holidays together growing up. They went to college together and still speak every day. He lives with his partner, Tristan, in Dana Point, California. He will be her shelter. He is very driven and will drag her along for the ride whether she wants him to or not. She looks up to him and admires his strength. He'll be critical to the healing process.

The priest delivers a beautiful homily. The gang goes over to our local watering hole, The Lantern. We spent many a night in that bar, shooting darts, sharing life stories, having one too many shots. I see them sit down at our usual table when the bartender sends them a complimentary Jägermeister shot, my go-to.

I'm a mix of emotions: sad, angry, and distraught, but mostly sentimental. I can't believe I'll never get to speak to them again, no more hugs, drinks . . . laughs. It's overwhelming to comprehend. I'm grateful for every treasured, memorable moment we have, but I wish I knew then what I know now. I would've stopped sweating the small stuff; I would've put aside the anxiety and worry to live each day to the fullest. I, somehow, need to convey this message to them so they don't waste their days on things they can't control.

#

Jake joins me as Hank pulls up to my parents's house. My mom invited her over to go through some of my things to see if she wants to keep anything. It's unbearable to watch everyone struggle through every painful second. With each breath, they question how they are still existing. Hank forces herself out of the car over to the front door. My mom greets her with a warm and loving embrace.

"Are you hanging in there, man?" Jake asks, grabbing my shoulder.

"My best friend is on her way into my house where my four siblings, spouses, niece and nephew, cousins, friends, and neighbors mourn my loss. Look around. My face is hanging on walls in every room. How will they ever recover?"

"They'll have to take it one day at a time. Sometimes, one minute at a time, but they will eventually find a new normal and get back to living. It will be excruciating, but they will get there, someday. That's the thing about death; it's permanent. Our loved ones need to realize they can't take anything for granted. Love can't be quantified; it's abounding, limitless — eternal. When you lose someone you love, sometimes we lose sight of nurturing all the other loving relationships in our lives, which is ironic. Maybe it's a defense mechanism. The fear of it happening again is so overwhelming that we begin to naturally distance ourselves. We go into hiding and shut down emotionally. Of course, everyone responds differently to grief. Healing must occur but the lesson in death should be to embrace life and all the beauty it creates. After all, nothing is guaranteed, and everything is temporary, even grief."

"Wow, you've only been here a few weeks and look at you with all the wisdom."

"Nah, just my coping mechanism." He pauses. "So, why don't you tell me about her."

"About who? *Hank?*" I watch as she enters my bedroom, inconsolable, begging for answers.

"Yeah. She's obviously carved deeply into your heart and soul."

"Man . . . to sum her up, she's everything. There was only one time I thought I might kiss her. We're hanging out at my house. She had too much to drink. My parents are out of town, so I insisted she sleep over. I don't want her driving. I help her up to my room and lead her to the adjoining twin bed in my room. When she lies down, she looks up at me with her sparkly, hazel green eyes. She looks so beautiful — sweet and innocent, entrusting me to take care of her. I know I make her feel safe. There is a split second where we lock eyes and all I want to do is kiss her so bad, but I don't want to ruin it. She's my best friend. What we have is once in a lifetime. I know how rare and special it is. I don't want to make a hasty decision all buzzed up, so I kiss her on the forehead and we never speak about it again."

"Dude, that's some serious will power."

"I grew up so much in that moment. I couldn't risk losing her and now she's lost me. I wish I would've savored and cherished everything more. High school, the concerts, all the laughing and silly inside jokes. Every bit of it." I watch her hand clinging to the claddagh necklace I bought her in Ireland for college graduation.

"I see that picture of the two of you on your dresser. When was the photo taken?" he asks, trying to distract me.

"Oh, that's from the John Mellencamp concert. We're huge fans. I took her to his show the summer after high school graduation. It was taken that night. Our favorite song is "Small Town." Ironically, one of the first things she asked me to do is to send her "Small

Town" to let her know I'm okay. It played on the jukebox at the bar, after the funeral earlier, during their toast to me. She's floored. I can tell she can sense me here. She can feel me around." We watch Hank as she wraps her arms around the frame, hugging it as hard as she can.

"Dan, you actually can hear me, can't you? What are the chances you would have this picture framed? It's like you were somehow leaving me breadcrumbs without even knowing it," Hank says.

"*See? It's* like she knows I'm right here talking about it and remembering, too."

"Yes, the more she gives in and listens, the stronger your connection will be. *HE* will tell you all about it when you meet," Jake informs me.

Hank continues to go through all my things in the closet. She saves my old, worn out Purdue sweatshirt, and a pair of my shiny, white Chuck Taylors. I haven't gone a day without wearing a pair since I met her unless there was a special occasion. She sorts through all the vinyl albums I collected over the years and stops at Neil Diamond. He's another one of our favorites. I chuckle, remembering walking up behind her and whispering, "*Did you ever read about a frog/ Who dreamed of bein' a king/ And then became one*"? The best line from the song "I Am . . . I Said."

"What's that?" Jake asks as Hank grabs a shoebox from under my bed.

"*Oh, shit!* I haven't even given a thought to Frank yet."

Hank finds the photo album of Frank and me from our Ireland trip.

"Who's Frank?"

"She's my college version of Hank, well, sort of. No one tops Hank but we were close. We went to Purdue together. Her name is Mary Christine Frances, but I call her Frank. She spent a semester abroad studying in France. I visited her, and we traveled to Ireland with Finn, her boyfriend at the time. The trip where I bought Hank that claddagh necklace. I got one for Frank, too. The last I heard, Frank stayed after college graduation to travel overseas then moved over to France permanently to be with Finn. I was so busy getting settled in with my life back here; we lost touch. She was never big on social media and I hadn't gotten around to getting in touch with her parents to get her contact information. Now, she might never know what happened."

"The puzzle will all make sense soon, my friend."

#

"Are you ready?" Jake asks as we approach the door to cross over.

"Ready as I'll ever be."

"Don't be nervous. Trust me, it only gets better from here," he reassures.

Believe it or not, I've grown fond of Jake the last few days. He's been a source of strength for me during this transition. It's comforting having someone here to guide me through it. I can tell that if our lives had crossed paths in the physical world, we would've been buds.

"Okay, on the count of three I want you to turn the handle," he says.

"Okay," I say, taking a deep breath.

"One . . . two . . . *three* . . . " he counts as I burst through the door. An enormous wave of adrenaline and euphoria blankets my body. Imagine the moment when you first fall in love, only it feels like you're floating in a never-ending river of it. Every pore of my skin is drinking it in, hydrating my soul. Goose bumps cover every inch of me. I feel tingly. The air is sweet, like the fold in the neck of a chubby baby right after a bath. It envelops me with endless warmth and sunshine. Birds are chirping. Angels are laughing and singing. Flowers are blooming. Rivers are flowing. Mountains as far as the eye can see. There are rainbows abounding with spectacular and vibrant, never seen before unearthly, colors. Pure bliss. Nothing I've *ever* experienced.

"*Well?*" Jake awaits my initial response.

"Speechless. It's nothing short of magical. There's no way to describe this in words alone."

"I know. I was sad to leave, even temporarily. You're going to love it here," he says.

"So, what's next?" I ask, trying to absorb everything.

"I'll show you around. Let's go check out our place."

Cars, buildings, retail stores and restaurants line the streets, but I can see forests and meadows off in the distance. People are everywhere but no one is in a hurry. There aren't any traffic signals or stop signs, no need. Everyone is polite, patient, peaceful, jolly, and content.

"We're going to live together?" I ask.

"Just until you get familiar with everything then you can go wherever, whenever you want. Remember, there is no such thing as defined space or time here.

Those are only parameters in the physical world. You have eternity to do everything you wish."

We enter the three-bedroom condominium located on the twelfth floor of a sixty-two-story building in the city center. The building is very modern, futuristic. The units cantilever over each other. Terraces extend from all sides. There's a lot of outdoor living here since the weather is perfect all the time. Our individual unit is open and airy. Floor to ceiling windows fill the space with bright, natural light overlooking the grand landscape. Floors are ceramic tile. The walls are painted in a perfect egg shell blue. Everything is automated and accessible from a remote control: all the appliances, overhead music system, electronic window treatments, and fireplace. Metal handrails with glass cutouts surround the sunken living room. It has an industrial feel but it's not cold. The furniture is oversized, comfortable and inviting. Everything is designed to encourage visitors.

"Three bedrooms?" I ask.

"Yes, they told me I'd have a roommate. We also have an extra room to use as an office for the work we'll be doing. It will serve as a guest room for anyone who wants to visit."

"*Wait*, can I have a girlfriend?"

"Yep. You can even get married. When most people get here, they reunite with their soulmate from the physical world, but since you never had one, your soulmate is already here."

"Wait, *she's here*? Really?" I ask in disbelief. "When can I meet her?"

"Slow your roll there buddy, you've got work to do," he says as I stake my claim to a bedroom. It's has a king-size bed; the bed's headboard has cut-out shelves for storage. Crisp white linen sheets and dozens of pillows. A walk-in closet and private spa bathroom. This is what I imagine I would live in as a bachelor. It's not oversized or overstated but more than sufficient. It's not like I brought anything with me.

#

"HE's the most laid-back guy you'll ever meet," Jake says as he opens the palatial gate for to me to enter the Roman Basilica Cathedral. It's the most divine place I've ever seen. More spectacular than any church I could dream up. The architecture is millions and millions of years old. The sprawling aisle leads up to the grandiose altar with arches framed in gold. The breathtaking columns, statues, and pews are carved with the finest detail. Stained glass windows surround the majestic dome. I'm in sheer awe.

"HIS office is up there next to the statue of Mary. Go knock. HE's expecting you," he says.

I haven't given this moment much thought. I mean, yes, I knew I'd meet HIM *someday* but not this early, so this never played out in my head. Ready or not, here I come. I take a deep breath as I approach the door and knock. I'm like a little kid on Christmas morning, anticipating the rush of joy, when HE opens the door.

"Welcome, Daniel, My son. I've been expecting you. Please come in," HE says, reaching out to greet me with a warm embrace then places a soft kiss on each cheek.

"*Oh my go . . . d . . .* gosh, *GOSH . . .* You look *exactly* like Your pictures. You're the spitting image of Jared Leto. It's uncanny . . . OR . . . I guess, he's the spitting image of You — right?" I laugh and give *HIM* a wink. "Sorry, sorry, I'm a little star struck here." *HE*'s six feet, medium build, and has the most beautiful blue eyes I've ever seen. *HE*'s wearing a beige cloth robe with a rope at the waist and Birkenstocks.

"Daniel, please come in and have a seat." *HE* escorts me to a cart table with two folding chairs. Suddenly, I feel like I'm walking to confession but it's *HIM*. *HE* already knows everything I've done and said, and *HE* let me in. There isn't anything I can tell *HIM*. *HIS* office looks like the basement of every church I've ever been in. I was expecting a massive throne with *HIS* disciples hustling around, waiting on *HIM* hand and foot, but *HE*'s alone.

"That is a fabulous work bench You have there," I say as we pass a room full of tools.

"Thank you. I use it every day. I love working with My hands . . . creating." *HE* grins.

"Ha. Good one. I wasn't sure if You'd be serious or if I could joke with You," I say with a smile.

"Daniel, I created you. I know you better than you know yourself. I gifted you with that sense of humor. It's one of My favorite things about you."

"Really? I apologize in advance if I ever did or said anything to offend You or use Your name in vain. It wasn't meant to hurt You."

"Ahh, it comes with the territory." *HE* laughs. As *HE*'s speaking, I realize how gentle, humble and gracious *HE* is.

"May I be candid?" I ask.

"*Please.*"

"You seem laid back for a guy with so much responsibility."

"I have a lot of time on My hands to practice patience. What other questions can I answer before we get down to why you're here?"

"Anything?"

"*Anything.*"

"Okay, rapid fire."

"How do You keep those sandals from smelling when Your feet sweat?"

"I have a new pair for each day."

"The robes, too?"

"Yep."

"How often do You get Your hair cut because it's perfection?"

"Once a week."

"Can You whistle?"

"Yes."

"*But,* can You whistle in German?" I pause as *HE* realizes the question. "*Ahhh,* gotcha on that one."

"You're very clever, Daniel, which is one of your most charming qualities. It's what I like to call your 'special sauce.' Most people wait a lifetime for this meeting. The most common question I get is 'Did I fulfill Your will?' You don't take yourself too seriously and I love that about you. You're still young. Life didn't have a chance to break you. Did you notice that you came into the world as an innocent being, without any preconceived notions or feelings? Life chips away at people's spirit with things like greed, control and judgement, which is why I need your help. But, before we dive into anything serious, there's one more thing I want to discuss."

"Of course."

"I know your big thing is to give people nicknames, so I want *you* to give *ME* one."

"Really? That's awesome. How about . . . " I pause. "*Chuy?*"

"Like *Chewbacca?*"

"Nooo, nooo. *Chuy* is an endearing nickname in the Spanish culture for *Jesus.*"

"*I love it!* From now on, no one else can call ME that but you; now let's get started."

CHAPTER THREE

"I know you're stunned to be here at such a young age, but I have important and influential work for you," *Chuy* says.

"You see, Daniel, you are one of the special ones. People are drawn to you. You're magnetic. You have a precious gift. You bring tremendous joy and happiness to everyone you encounter with your vivacious spirit. You make them feel comfortable in their own skin. You bring them a sense of light-heartedness where they feel joyous and cheerful, which is why this journey will continue over here, for eternity. You have endless joy to spread. This is also the reason why the loss is going to be excruciating for your loved ones. You've left a deep impact and now a bottomless void exists forever, but there is one person who will suffer and carry this . . ."

"*Hank.*"

"Yes, she is one of your soulmates, your kindred spirit, not in a romantic way, but your souls were connected long before your meeting. They know and love each other deeply. She is crippled at the thought of not having you with her throughout her lifetime. Your loss is debilitating to her. However, she is destined for amazing things, which is why you're here. I have one job for you. Once you're successful at fulfilling this role, countless people will be impacted."

"Of course, yes, I'm up for the task. I want nothing more than to help my loved ones heal so I'll do anything You ask, whatever it takes."

"I need you to convince Hank this place exists. She needs to believe, *without a doubt*, that eternity exists, and I know *you* are the only one who can ever get through to her."

"*Whhaat*?? What about You?"

"Nope. She won't listen to Me. She's stubborn. But she trusts *you*. She misses *you*. She is searching for answers and *you* are the only one who can provide them." My mind races. Hank and I never talked about death, but she does have amazing intuition. She could predict the outcome of things before they happened. It's like a sixth sense. I never put much stock in it, but maybe there's something to this.

"Here's the catch — you're only allowed to communicate with her through signs and symbols."

"Like a billboard that says, 'HANK, *it's real, I'm here, I swear. Get over it, love you, see you soon. XO*'?"

"My job would have been done millions upon millions of years ago if it were that simple. No, signs like special songs, license plates, repeating numbers, electricity flickering, birds, butterflies, dragonflies, animals that grab her attention, feathers and pennies — things along these lines."

"How am I going to do that if I don't have *Your* powers? Oh my go . . dSH, sorry, *sorry*, I keep forgetting." I stumble. "Are You going to give me Your powers for a day, like Jim Carey in the movie *Bruce Almighty*?"

"No. Every Angel is equipped with these subtle abilities. You'll know every move she is going to make before she makes it, so you will know the things that will be in her path."

"Hmmm, okay . . . " I pause. "I have a couple clarifying questions."

"Of course."

"Am I allowed to trip her?"

"No."

"Push her?"

"Nope."

"How about just a gentle slap if she's *really* not getting it?"

"Negative."

"I don't mean to be difficult, but I can tell You right now this is a colossal waste of time. It's never going to work, so good thing You're giving me an eternity to accomplish it. It will be like a permanent *Groundhog Day* situation. Hank won't listen; she's not focused, and she's a doubting Thomas. She'll question every little thing."

"Tell *ME* about it. I'm relinquishing the job of convincing her over to you. *Remember? Whatever it takes.* Here's the deal. She wants, more than anything, to hope again. She's already researching for ways to communicate with you."

"Ohhhh, wait." I stop, thinking about how I can turn this into a fun game. "Can we give her a code name?"

"Sure, what would you like to call h . . ?"

"*Dory*," I interrupt. "Operation Dory, as in Dory from *Finding Nemo*. Hank has the shortest memory of anyone I know. No matter how grand the sign or gesture will be, ten minutes later, she'll need constant reassurance. I haven't even started, and I know this. No question."

"You're correct, which is why you're assigned to her 24/7 because I don't have time. Your task is to rebuild her inner strength and confidence, to grow her faith so she believes in all the possibilities. You see, she lost all her courage and bravery when she lost you. Now she's afraid to take risks, to live and love again at the fear of losing another great love in her life. She's tentative, cautious, timid, and fearful. She won't act on her instincts. She'll retreat to a comfortable, safe place to protect herself."

"So, wait. . . let me get this straight. She gets her *own* full-time, dedicated angel because she is so high maintenance?"

"*Technically*, yes. You have her, and I have the *rest* of the world, but it's because she is destined for *big* things. She is another chosen one. She will chase all the wrong things. Things that she can predict or situations that appear to have a guaranteed outcome in her favor, so she'll stumble, fall and fail. These will all be dead ends which will cause her to retreat even more. It will shatter her. This is your window. Hopelessness and despair are the only catalysts to change. Safety is the death of greatness. She needs to be uncomfortable. She will look to you to guide her and give her answers. It's the only path to recovery. She will heal and overcome, knowing you're with her every step of the way. Once you convince her to believe, without a doubt, the sky's the limit for her. It's going to lead her to her greater purpose. She's going to write about her experience. She's meant to be a writer. That's her gift. You are her muse and inspiration. You'll lead her there. She'll document all the signs and describe the guidance you send her *and* it's going to catch on like wildfire. Through her journey, she'll convince countless others their loved ones are with them, too. They'll start paying attention to the signs they receive, and so on. Here's the best part. She dedicates the entire story to you and your friendship."

"Aww, really?"

"Yes. Once she trusts again, she is going to persuade numerous, living souls, that all of *this* is real," HE says, gesturing to our surroundings. "That *I'm* real, that we're here and it's only a matter of time before we're all here together, forever. She's in tune. She senses you're around. You're spot on; it's going to take *a lot* of convincing, so be patient with her. Her ability to see, hear and feel you will grow the more she believes. You'll have to try different tactics to try to get through to her. Some things will work better than others."

"Are there any special rules?" I ask.

"You can find ME at any time, but we will only have three formal meetings during this process. This is the first." HE hands me a hard-covered journal with an inscription, *The Man Guide*. "You can document your experience in here, between our meetings. You keep this journal for Hank, of the lessons she has to learn in the physical world, so when she gets here all of her questions will be answered around the major events that occurr in her life."

"What does the engraving signify?"

"That is for you to discover during the process. Also, you get *one* super sign. This is called a visitation. You must save it for the perfect moment. You can visit her in a dream and speak to her, but she will not remember details of the encounter. Her subconscious will. She will have déjà vu moments where things will come into focus."

"Did someone keep a journal for me?"

"No, because you weren't struggling for answers. You were content. You lived life to the fullest. I made you special because you only had a short time to leave an impression. Journals start when individuals begin to doubt, when they hit a crossroads and they're not listening." *HE* pauses. "So, are you up for the challenge? From this point forward, all your physical world emotions will be gone. You will only experience happiness, apart from our meetings. When we're together, you can express any emotion," *Chuy* says.

"What about the rest of my friends and family? Can I see them?"

"Of course, you can support all of them. Remember there isn't any space or time here, so you can be anywhere at any time, which is the perfect segue. Another one of your friends will be joining you here soon." *HE* pauses. "Your friend, Frank."

"Oh no. What's wrong with Frank?" I ask as *HE* holds my hand and we go to her. Finn is with her.

"She and Finn are about to get married. She'll soon get pregnant but will suffer a miscarriage. When they go in for the procedure, they will find cancer. She will suffer from Stage III breast and ovarian cancer. The doctors will have to perform a hysterectomy. They will, of course, be heartbroken. She'll go through aggressive treatment and reach remission, but it will be only temporary, about eighteen months. Then it will spread to her bones and be just matter of time. You'll be the one to greet her when she arrives to help her to transition here. Christine's husband Finn will be just as destroyed as Hank."

"This is *horrifying*. They have no idea the grief that lies ahead. At least with my loved ones, they didn't have time to worry or anticipate. In a sense, you ripped the bandage off."

"There is no easy way, Daniel. Loss in any form is an immense shock to those in the physical world. You, Jake, and Christine will be the new three musketeers. You're all tasked with the same job — guiding your loved ones to their true destiny. You know what's best for them, so I will let you devise the plan. Just remember, they'll be tested. Free will works against them until they are in harmony with the universe. Once they start following their true path, doors will open. Most people never find it. They go through life going through the motions. Each person is brought into the world with a special gift; it's up to them to discover it. My only request is to exercise patience, waiting for them to wake up and realize the possibilities. In the meantime, you'll get to live life through their eyes."

"When is our next meeting?" I ask.

"We don't schedule these. You'll know when it's time." *HE* smiles and retreats to his workshop.

#

"*Well?*" Jake asks when greeting me outside the church.

"*Chuy is incredible.* Did you get one of these?" I ask, showing him my journal.

"Yes. Who's *Chuy?*"

"Oh, *HE* let me give *HIM* a nickname. *Chuy* is a loving term for Jesus in the Spanish culture," I reply. "What is the imprint on yours?"

"Oh, nice. Mine says *The Journey.* Why don't you tell me all about the meeting while I show you around?

Let's grab a beer. I want to take you to my favorite local pub, McGee's," he says.

"Sounds heavenly." I wink.

We spend the rest of the day exploring the scene. I fill him in on Frank's untimely arrival. When we get home, I go to my room to write my first letter to Hank.

\#

ENTRY #1

My Beloved Hank,

I have SO much to tell you!!!!!!

First, I miss you endlessly! It pains me to know how much everyone is struggling with unfathomable sadness. If you could only see where I am, you wouldn't spend another ounce of time worrying, fretting, or trying to make sense of this seemingly senseless tragedy. I'm in a better place, no . . . the BEST place. Something that is so indescribable it must be experienced firsthand. The beauty is expansive. The sun shines so bountifully that the glare off the lakes and rivers sparkles like diamonds. Trees bloom with luscious bushels of flowers, fruitful with the scent of lavender. Colors are so deep and rich, they embrace you like a warm blanket while taking your breath away. The depth of love is immeasurable. There isn't any pain, suffering or sadness. There is only joy and abundance.

Secondly, I want you to know how much I love you. You are, and will always be, my very best friend. Nothing will ever change that. I can still see and hear you. You just can't see or hear me. I need you to do me a HUGE favor. You must concentrate on two different senses — hearing and touch. You need to listen for me and feel me. I will always be with you. I'm the whistle in the wind, the breath on your check, the warmth in every hug, and the light in your heart and soul. I need you to trust me now more than ever, okay? I promise you, I'll be here every single step of the way, leading you to your destiny. Focus on the signs.

Lastly, I met the big guy. HE assigned me to you. HE even let me give HIM a nickname. It's Chuy. HE's the most humble, gentle, kind, and generous person you'll ever be lucky enough to meet. HE gave me this journal, so I can capture these moments and life lessons for you.

I made a friend here — Jake. You'll really like him. He's chill. I can tell we'll be good pals here.

Anyway, more soon.

I love you forever and always,

Danny

CHAPTER FOUR

"Jake, do you want to come with me? Hank is meeting Red for lunch today. She's going to introduce the 'spirit' topic with her. This should get interesting and I want a front row seat," I say.

"Oh, this should be fun. I'm *in*," he responds as we make our way to the restaurant.

"Did I tell you Hank is keeping a journal of her own? She's documenting her requests to me — for signs. She's still open to the possibility that I'm around. She talks to me every day and visits me at the cemetery as often as she can, but never misses a Saturday. Until today, she's been holding these details close to the vest. She's protecting herself. She's fearful of being judged. She doesn't want anyone to think she's gone over the deep end, so she's being cautious. I can tell she's about to burst. She wants to confide in Red to gain some perspective and validation. Red will be open to it."

"Maybe this will be easier than you think," Jake adds.

Red approaches the table where Hank, Jake and I are already seated. This is my first real outing as a "spirit," so I'm enjoying observing my surroundings. It's a cute café set up like a bistro. The shoulder-high counter display in the entrance is full of gourmet pastries. The air is filled with the aroma of freshly brewed coffee, cinnamon pastries mixed with french fries. It's an intimate space. Tables are just a few inches apart with a couple of long picnic-like tables for community seating. A handful of people are dining alone. There's an older couple enjoying the hustle and bustle of their surroundings. A moment ago, I would've been like any one of these patrons, sitting in this restaurant without a care in the world. I'd be reading the menu and deciding between the Reuben sandwich and the chicken, bacon, and avocado panini. Decisions would be made in four-hour increments. *Should I go to a movie, get an oil change, or go back home and take a nap before going out tonight? I never understand the urgency, importance or privilege of what it means to be here. Do any of these folks know their world could turn upside down in an instant? Do they appreciate the little things? I realize now how much I take for granted. How many days did I spend with Hank, Red and our other buddies assuming there would be endless days to come? I didn't fully appreciate the warmth of her hug, the sparkle in her eye, the sweetness of her laugh, or her endless naivety and innocence. It's no wonder she's broken. Everything she believes in and trusts is ripped away in the blink of an eye. I must get through to her. C'mon, Hank. We can do this.*

"Where did you come from?" Red asks, embracing Hank.

"The cemetery. Visiting Dan," Hank replies.

"Aww. That's sweet. You should've told me. I would've met you there."

"You can join me any Saturday you like. It's become a regular thing."

"*Really?* Why didn't you tell me?"

"I don't want anyone to think I've lost it because fifty percent of the people I talk to on a regular basis are dead. But it comforts me to be there."

"I get that," Red assures as the waitress approaches the table to introduce herself and the daily specials.

Little do they both know, we're sitting *right here* . . . in the seat between them. Red orders the soup of the day and a spinach salad. Hank orders a bottle of wine to gain the liquid courage to ask Red her thoughts and feelings on psychics and mediums. She starts beating around the bush. *C'mon, Hank, spit it out. She's your best friend . . . and it's me we're talking about it. She'll get it.*

"I've had some weird things happen. You could say coincidences, but I think it's more than that." She pauses.

"Like what?"

"A couple days after Dan died I was going through boxes of my memorabilia and I found this postcard he sent me back in college, which I've been carrying with me ever since." She hands it over the table to Red.

"Liv, this is — this is crazy. Look at the name of the song he's referencing — 'If I Die Sudden.'"

"I know. It took my breath away."

"Liv . . . I just got chills." Red's eyes fill up with tears.

"What are the chances? I mean, really? That I would have something in writing from him that would not only reference a Mellencamp song, but the title of it almost predicting his fate?"

"Speechless," she says with a stunned reaction.

"Even crazier? I asked him to try to communicate with me through music, to send me 'Small Town' anytime I need to feel him with me. Remember the night at the bar after the funeral, as we were toasting to him, it came on?"

"Yes. Okay, now you are creeping me out."

"I know it's really hard to grasp but every ounce of my being believes it's Dan trying to connect with me. Think about it. We were at The Lantern, the last place

I ever saw him, toasting to his life and 'Small Town' starts playing, and after I just asked him for it. There is no way that's a coincidence. Not a chance."

"Unbelievable." She sits back in her chair in disbelief as a young man approaches the table.

Oh, this should be good. Go ahead, dude, introduce yourself. Bring it home.

"Excuse me, ladies. Sorry to interrupt. I'm Daniel. I'm helping out your waitress this afternoon. She asked me to clarify if you want the dressing on your salad or on the side?"

Dumbfounded, they reply almost mesmerized, "On . . . the . . . side."

"Okay . . . thank you," he says awkwardly as he heads back to the kitchen.

"SEE?" Hank bursts. "This is exactly what I'm talking about."

"Liv, this is overwhelming."

"If you didn't know me better, you'd think I paid that kid to come over here to prove my point."

"You're right. This is beyond belief."

"Well, not so fast, there is a third thing, too."

"I don't know if I can handle it," she says, running her hands through her hair, trying to absorb everything Hank is telling her.

"Leaving the cemetery today, I pulled up to the light behind a car with the license plate *HUGS*."

"*Stop it.* That's insane."

"I know. I did some research on guardian angels and messages. The sources seem legitimate and it's consistent across the board. From what I've read, it states angels communicate through symbols like songs, license plates, birds, butterflies, rainbows, feathers, pennies, and meaningful numbers like birthdays or any double numbers like 11:11 or 4:44. It's not only that you see or hear these things but it's about when. They are directing your attention to these things, so you know they're with you. Like today, leaving his grave site and seeing that license plate. How did my mind not only see it but register what it said? It happened in such a flash."

"I'm not going to lie; in the beginning, I was skeptical but you made me a believer," Red says as the waitress arrives with their food.

Still stunned from their Dan interruption, Hanks says, "Okay, well, I'm only sharing this with you. So, can we please keep it our secret?"

"Your secret is safe with me and, Liv, I really do hope it is true . . . for you."

Boom, there it is. Yes, YES. It's real. It's all real. I promise.

"She's identified the signs, straight from *Chuy's* mouth," I say.

"Wow. That's amazing. Hank has the whole formula figured out," Jake comments. "So, what's missing?"

"*Time,*" I respond. "She's going to require more of that, than anything, but Red is here to deliver an important message of her own. She's here to try to convince Hank to join the Second City to take improv writing classes. Hank is funny. She's always been a great storyteller. Hands down, the funniest chick I know."

"Really? I know a couple of those myself," Jake adds.

"Yes, and I know funny. Red is the *only* one who can convince her to take this leap. Red misses the old Hank. My death has her paralyzed. I stole her fun-loving, carefree inner spirit. *Chuy* shared that Hank's destiny is to become a writer. Second City is the first step in this process for her. It's the perfect recipe. Strangers will help her to slowly open-up again. She'll meet new people, but they won't know anything about this burden that she carries. She will only share the parts of herself where she won't feel exposed or vulnerable. Since she won't be fully invested in them, she can keep them at arm's length and protect herself by maintaining emotional distance. She'll experiment and compartmentalize while she tries to find her new normal. Improv is the place where she can tap back into her creativity and learn the tools to connect with that energy. During this adventure, she'll come across some influential people important to her future in the business."

"All right, go Red! Let's do *this*," Jake adds.

"Not so fast. Here's the catch. She's going to throw a wrench into everything. The visions have started. The ones where I can see into the future. In a few weeks, she's going to get rip-roaring drunk and have her first, and only, one-night stand with one of the guest instructors, Malcolm Hill. He's not only famous but also happens to be her future husband's best friend." I pause. "Did you get all of that?"

"*Wait, what?*"

"Exactly, just wait. You'll notice a common theme throughout her journey. She'll be her biggest obstacle."

#

"Oh. My. Goodness. *Dan, is that you?*" Frank asks as I greet her in the waiting room.

"Yes, Frank, it's me," I say as we embrace.

"What on *earth* are you doing here? Or should I say, *good heavens!*" she smiles.

"I got here not too long after we graduated. It was a car accident. Hit head on," I reply.

"Oh my gosh. Your family must be devastated. I had no idea. I never heard. I tried reaching out to you when we got engaged then, well, life happened."

"Yes, it's been a difficult road for them, especially Hank."

"Oh, poor Hank! Poor thing. I'm so glad I didn't know."

"Hank found the photo album of us from our travels through Ireland with Finn. She vowed not to find you because she didn't want you to live in a world where I didn't exist."

"Aww, how sweet. I'm not going to lie. I couldn't have hoped for a better, more loving face to welcome me. You make having to be here . . . worth it," she says.

"You're going to love this place and you're not even there yet. I'll be with you every step of the way." I fill her in on the next steps and we get caught up on all our lost time.

"Finn is who I'm most worried about," she says.

She met Finn when studying abroad her last semester in France. I knew the minute I met him in Ireland: He was a stand-up guy. Great dude. Handsome, I mean, not as handsome as me but attractive. He's uber-talented and always took excellent care of her. I'd trust him with any girl, including one of my sisters. He's from St. Andrew's, Scotland. He was attending culinary school in Paris when he and Frank first met. Malcolm Hill — Mac, is Finn's best childhood friend. Mac left Scotland at the same time as Finn to pursue a comedy career. He moved to New York when he was selected to join the Second City's comedy review. Mac was a bit of a 'ladies' man, hence the random hook up with Hank, but quickly settled down after meeting Jules at Frank's wedding. Jules is Frank's best pal from home. Frank and Finn were living in his parents's retirement flat in Paris when she got sick. Once things took a turn for the worse, they moved back to the US to live with her parents in their small town in Indiana. They came with the hopes of participating in a last ditch clinical trial, with a company called Hellyxia. A couple of years ago they released a state of the art clinical drug called Brcaxia, focused solely on curing women with the BRCA1 gene. This new drug was the first of its kind in the marketplace. It was bleeding-edge, revolutionary medicine and reported a high success rate. Unfortunately, Frank's disease was too far along for her to qualify so she lived out the rest of her days with Finn and her parents by her side.

We spend the next few days witnessing the grueling process of her beloved friends and family laying her to rest.

#

ENTRY #2

My beloved Hank,

This is even harder than I imagined. Being so close to you but you not believing I'm here. I've heard every single word, each plea and prayer. I've caught every tear drop and want nothing more than to hug you and let you know it's all going to be okay. I promise. Have faith. I know you want to, but you're scared. Please. I'm begging you. You need to learn to let go and allow me to guide you. I will never leave you. I will always protect you from harm. You keep getting in your own way. You'll continue to be your own worst enemy and I'll continue to do everything in my power to convince you I'm here.

I'm proud of you for taking the leap and joining Second City. You have no idea what's in store for you. Big things. Amazing things. I'll keep leaving breadcrumbs. One day at a time. One step at a time.

Oh, and you're never going to believe it — Frank is here, too. You'll find out the details eventually but I'm glad to have a partner in crime here. She and I are about to start plotting some BIG things up here. Stay tuned.

Anyway, more soon.

I love you forever and always,

Danny

P.S. And yes, I did witness the whole naked-Mac-one-night-stand-drunkfest. You'll definitely regret that decision. #notpretty.

CHAPTER FIVE

I greet Frank outside the church after her meeting with *Chuy*.

"How was it?" I ask, already knowing it was nothing short of epic.

"Beyond incredible." She turns the cover of her journal towards me. It's inscribed, *The Gift*. "HE told me these words will reveal their meaning throughout Finn's healing process."

She fills me in on the rest of the meeting as we head back to my place to introduce her to Jake.

"Hi, Frank, such a pleasure to meet you. I've heard so much about you," Jake says. "How exciting was it to see this mug waiting for you at the pearly gates?"

"Truly the best thing ever," she smiles.

"Can I convince you to stay here with us? We'd love to have you. You can have my room; I'll take the spare room," I offer.

"Are you sure?"

"Yes, absolutely. We wouldn't have it any other way." I show her around. I can tell from her reaction she'll fit in just fine here.

"Next stop, McGee's," Jake says.

McGee's is open all day, every day. Nothing closes here. You can go anywhere you want whenever you want. No inconveniences, hassles or waiting. Everything is available at your fingertips. I realize this might seem over the top, but I assure you, it's not. *Chuy* never wants any soul to ever go without, ever again. *HE* doesn't go to extremes but remember there are no human emotions here. No greed, jealousy or envy. No one is devoid of or in competition for anything, including attention. There is no desire to be better, richer or smarter than anyone else. Everyone is accepted and loved for exactly who they are. *Chuy* wants to offer a little bit of everything for us to enjoy. The best way to describe it here is to say it's just enough. We sit at our regular table and order a round.

"I guess I'll dive right in," Frank says.

"Go for it," I say.

"Obviously, the last couple years have been rough for Finn and me. We lost the baby only to find out that I had cancer and we see how that turned out. I'm Finn's first love. He's so young to experience such a tremendous loss. He doesn't know how to navigate this. He's not equipped with the tools to cope. He's been utterly shattered into pieces. I don't know how he is going to ever move on. Before I left, I told him I would send him signs, like butterflies and rainbows, to let him know I was okay."

"That's incredible. I had no idea about these signs until I met with *Chuy* and *HE* told me all about them. Hank did research about ways to communicate with me and these are some of the most common symbols *HE* mentioned."

"That's not at all what I did. I wrote Finn a letter, well, two letters, and told him when he's ready for love again to go searching for . . . wait for it . . . HANK!"

"*Whaaaaaat?*"

"Yup. He doesn't know anything about it. I left the letter with my mom and told her when the time is right she should give it to him. He obviously needs plenty of time to heal, but, eventually, I hope he'll be in a place where he's ready. He'll dive into his work and he won't put himself out there."

"All I can say is W.O.W!"

"Believe it or not, Jake — Hank and I never met in person," Frank adds.

"You've *got* to be kidding me."

"No, it wasn't intentional. It just never happened. There wasn't any opportunity which leads me to my next question. How did you pick Hank without knowing her?" I ask.

"The only endorsement I need is watching the way you light up when you're talking about her. She's hands down your favorite person. Even I can't compete with that. On top of it, she's incredibly beautiful, inside and out, and she's *funny*. He'll need someone to make him laugh."

"That's accurate. I'm touched and honored. I'm surprised, though. Don't get me wrong, it's an incredible idea. She does deserve the best and, believe it or not, I had the *exact same idea*. I was going to wait a little longer to share. I thought I'd give you a hot minute to settle in before I stole your widowed husband for my best friend," I say.

"Not at all. I'm thrilled to know you think Finn is just as worthy," she responds. "They both have extraordinary hearts. Hearts without borders which allows them to love unconditionally. Coupled with that gift is the burden of grief they face now having lost us. Neither will fully recover on their own. They need to find each other. Only then will they begin to repair the insurmountable valley torn within their hearts."

"I have to say, I think it's so dope you're willing to spend eternity guiding them toward each other."

"It's not going to be easy. We still have free will to contend with," Frank says.

"*And* Hank," I add. "I hope you still like her by the time I get through to her."

"Okay, back to these letters. I want to hear what they say," Jake says, trying to bring us back into focus.

"That's easy. I remember every word." She continues speaking.

#

LETTER #1

My dearest Finn,

I don't want you to be sad for me. I'm in a beautiful place; a place where there is no pain or suffering. A place where there is no time, only love in the truest form. I hope you've taken the time you need to grieve and given yourself space to heal, but what I want most is to know you are living a life of abundance. I hope you're reading this and your heart and soul are full and happy. My biggest wish for you is to find your next true soul mate. Someone beautiful who makes your heart soar, who makes you want to get out of bed every morning and live; someone who will love you without limits. Someone who sees your beautiful gifts and treasures every moment she gets to spend with you. Know that I did not ever want to leave you, but this is all part of God's plan. I will be watching over you and sending you signs to let you know I am right here with you always. God has big plans for you. HE took me early because HE needs me with HIM, but there's nothing but great things in store for you. Trust me.

I love you forever,

Christine

#

LETTER #2

Finn,

Okay, this one is a little more lighthearted . . . First, please give my girl Jules the biggest hug imaginable and tell her how much I love and miss her. I will be watching over her, too, and will always be close, she's my best friend, I won't ever leave her, and we're soul sisters.

So, if you haven't found someone yet, do me a favor and look this girl up. Her name is Olivia Henry. You can probably find her on social media. She lives in Chicago. She's Dan's best friend from high school. He loved her as much as he loved me, only more. Anyway, I never met her, but he never dated either one of us, which is miraculous. He always said she is spectacular, and spectacular is right up your alley. Plus, clearly, he has good taste in the women he chooses to share his company with. Nothing like getting dating advice from your dead wife, huh?

Love you, Christine XO

"Those are wonderful. Is now the appropriate time to tell you that Hank had a one-night stand with Mac?" I blurt.

"*What?*" she responds.

"Yep." I pause. "They did the dirty."

"Oh my gosh. How is that even possible? Wait, *did he cheat on Jules?*"

"No, no, nothing like that. It was a random one-night drunken thing before they ever met." I explain the circumstances.

"Phew, but what are the chances?" she comments.

"I know, right?"

"I guess we really do have our work cut out for us," she says then shifts the conversation.

"Jake, I feel like we're being so rude. I've asked nothing about you. Here you are, sitting and listening to Danny and I outline our grand plans. Tell me your story," she encourages.

"Well, I got here just before Dan. Same deal. Car accident. I went to the University of Kentucky. Grew up in Fort Thomas, Kentucky. I had one younger sister, Tricia."

"I'm so sorry," Frank says.

"Yes, obviously we're all in the same boat. We're in a majestic place but desperate to connect with our loved ones to let them know we're okay. I'm grateful to have both of you."

"As are we, my friend," I say, raising a glass to toast our new friendship. "To the three musketeers!"

"So, tell me something interesting about yourself?" Frank asks.

"Dan and I have compared notes and we both share a deep love of music. Several of the same bands. One of my favorite songs of all time is "Desire" by U2. I used to drive my friend Liza crazy by screaming it at the top of my lungs at the back of study hall in high school."

"Tell her about the panty check," I prod.

"Dude, don't make me seem like a pervert right out of the gate. Frank barely knows me."

"I can't help it. This is too good. She knows my shenanigans far too well and I'm really that jealous I never thought to use it. It's brilliant."

"So, every day at school I'd go up behind all my girlfriends and grab their butts for a 'pantycheck.' I told them I was helping them out to ensure we couldn't see any panty lines." He waits for her response then adds, "I mean, not in a creepy way . . . it was all in good fun."

"*Uh huh*, I know your type. You're so innocent and disarming . . . girls can't help but cave in to your charm. I get it," she says as we all laugh.

"Never. *EVER*. I have so much respect for women. I have a sister. I'd never do anything to embarrass her. I'd kill anyone that put her in a position where she would feel uncomfortable," he clarifies.

"I'm just teasing you. I can tell you're harmless. Relax." She reaches over to rub his back to offer further assurance.

"Tell her your favorite part of a girl's body. . . "

"*Dude*. Seriously, you're killing me here. *Ugh*. I don't know, there's something sexy about watching a girl as she gets out of the swimming pool. The water dripping off her body. The first thing they do is take their index fingers and run them down their hip to the back of their leg to ensure their bathing suit bottoms are providing full coverage, if you know what I'm saying."

"So, what you're saying is you're an ass man?" Frank jokes.

"Can we *please* change the subject?" Jake begs.

"Enough torturing you for the time being," I say. "Let's go back to Finn. What's next for him?"

"Well, he's still in the States, closing up from the funeral at my parents' house. He's not going to have the strength to go back to our place in Paris, at least not in the short term. Mac and Jules know him as well as I do. They know the only way he'll survive is to distract himself. He needs to dive into his passion — cooking. They've invited him back to stay with them, for a week or so, in New York where they're living while they film Mac's sitcom," Frank says.

"Wow, he's made quite the name for himself," I say.

"Yes, the Second City gig led him to an exciting career in network television. He's the lead in one of the most popular TV shows, *Roommates*."

"Nice."

"Yeah and it's perfect timing. The director and producer of Mac's show are about to start filming a reality cooking competition, called *Delectable*. They're going to trick Finn into auditioning for it."

"How so?"

"Mac will invite Finn to the set to keep him distracted and tell him their catering services team dropped the ball, so they need his help cooking for the cast. Mac knows he needs to spring this whole concept on him. He'd never agree to it. It's a twelve-week competition, shooting in Brooklyn, so he'll be close to Mac and Jules in the short term."

"Terrific idea."

"What about Hank? How's she doing?" she asks.

"Well, after the whole Mac situation, she bailed on her classes at Second City. Her sister, Jane, just gave birth to twins — Livey and Owen — whom she is obsessed with, which is adorable. She even made a deal with me. She said she would gladly forego marriage if I promise to watch over and keep them safe. *Ummm, crazy much?* Of course, I'm going to watch over them. They are her pride and joy. I'll do whatever I have to to fiercely protect them. She's so paranoid with e-v-e-r-y-t-h-i-n-g since I left. She treats everything like a horse trade. She doesn't think she can have it all. She lives in constant fear of something bad happening, always waiting for the other shoe to drop, which makes it that much more crucial for me to convince her I'm here."

"That's horrible," Frank laments.

"Oh, no, I haven't gotten to the horrible part yet. Not long after the twins were born, she was at her annual corporate meeting in San Francisco and had an epiphany to tell everyone, in her drunken state, that she quit."

"Oh no," Frank says.

"Oh *yes*. She could have gotten the job back if she really wanted, but she needed some serious downtime to regroup. She's currently on what will end up being a yearlong sabbatical."

"Wow. Good for her."

"I wish I had the balls to quit a job. Talk about epic!" Jake adds.

"Oh, Hank is full of surprises. You haven't even begun to witness *epic* yet."

#

ENTRY #3

My beloved Hank,

I know you're struggling. Please, please, please trust me. I'm doing everything in my power to pull strings up here. I'll take you where you need to be. Stay open to my messages. Frank and I are about to weave a very large web where you will be captured — in the best way possible. Try to have some fun along the way. I promise it is well worth the wait.

Anyway, more soon.

I love you forever and always,

Danny

CHAPTER SIX

Frank and I spread out in the living room to get down to business. We have gobs of planning to do to ensure Hank and Finn's lives intersect at the perfect moment. No small effort, considering they don't even know the other one exists. Both need time to heal, so we can't have it happen before they're ready and open to it. Trickier than it seems. Mix in a bowl of free will and it becomes even more of a complicated formula. In fact, our only objective is to ensure all the dead ends lead them to each other. Consider us coaches. Our job is to course correct through a multitude of persuasion tactics.

We don't necessarily know or care about what's happened in the past. We want to ensure the lesson was learned from those experiences. We can, however, see into the future. We can anticipate our loved one's choices and predict the outcome. Our influence is limited to the signs we send, and their interpretation gleaned from them. We cannot impact free will in any way, shape or form. Therefore, our job is extra challenging. Our biggest obstacle is human emotion. People tend to lead from their head, not their heart. Intuition is a real thing. You need to trust it.

"Let's get comfortable." Frank hands me a canister of markers and a stack of sticky notes. The adhesive will allow us to move things around. We'll use the glass windows as our backdrop. And with that, the plotting begins. Jake is off tending to his family, so we have the place to ourselves.

"Let's start with Hank since she's the wild card," I suggest.

"Sounds good," Frank agrees.

"Let's start with outlining the six major categories: job, life's purpose, family, friends, love, and me. I'll be the overarching grouping. I'm critical to each one of these areas and will be prepared to step in, at any point, to help further guide Hank along the path we're leading her down. Let's start with the job. Hellyxia. . . "

"No way. That's the company that was going to perform my clinical trial of Brcaxia, but I didn't qualify," she interrupts.

"Bingo. This company is *shady*. It's run by a bunch of unethical, heartless douchebags. They're only in it for one thing — the bottom line."

"Is that why I couldn't get in for treatment?" Frank asks.

"One of the reasons. For them, it's strictly a numbers game. They want to serve patients with the best insurance benefits, who have the highest odds of a long-term survival rate. That said, you should know that there wasn't any real cure to save your strain of the disease. The treatment may have bought you a few more months, but you'd still be here."

"Well, that makes me feel a little better knowing my fate wasn't in someone else's hands, other than *Chuy*, if dying was inevitable. So why Hellyxia?"

"Because Hank will be enamored with the cause. They'll throw a fancy executive title at her. She'll get drawn into being associated with the cure. After the interview, they'll have her hook, line and sinker. She'll ignore the red flags, initially, which is our ticket to getting her in the door. In most situations, she tends to view things at face value. She gives everyone the same benefit of the doubt. Things will bubble up once she is immersed in the culture. The executive personalities will start to reveal themselves and her claws will come out. If there's one thing I can guarantee about Hank, she will not be backed into a corner."

"Nobody puts baby in the corner!" Frank laughs.

"Exactly. Don't mistake her kindness or sweetness as weakness. She'll come out swinging and I guarantee, you'll lose. As open and warm hearted as she is, she is grounded in her convictions. She leads with authenticity and integrity. She's no push over. If she smells a rat, she'll eat them alive," I say.

"I love it. A girl after my own heart — fierce. Good for her," Frank says.

"It takes a lot to get on her bad side but *ooof*, when you do . . . it is not fun for anyone."

"So, what's going to happen at the job?"

"She's going to blow the place up, well, figuratively. I'll give you a front row seat to that shit show *but* she's going to quit. Which leads me to my next topic. Family. The second her job implodes, she's going to go straight to the airport to seek refuge at her cousin Garrett's house in Palm Springs, California. He is her safety net. She will need him to shelter her from the backlash of her impulsive decisions. She'll arrive during the midst of planning for the grand opening of his new store Gin & Tonic . . ."

"Oh, I get it now. That's *the window*. The timing is perfect because once Finn wins the reality show competition, he'll go off to Vegas to run the restaurant Mint for a year, per the contract. By then he'll have built the restaurant, Christine's, in Palm Springs."

". . . who Garrett will hire to cater his grand opening," I finish.

"This is fantastic," she says.

"We'll need to sprinkle in on-going encouragement from her friends and family to further support our cause, but this should line up nicely," I say. "She'll be so disgusted with Corporate America, she'll literally do anything to avoid going back to a 'job.' Once she starts to relax and meets Finn, the love of her life, her priorities will shift. His passion for cooking will create a spark and drive her to find her bigger purpose. He'll bring out the best in her and *voilà* — she'll start to write."

"Fate. Destiny. Serendipity. How do people not understand these are real? How do they not know we are real? They downplay it, brush it off and say, it's just coincidence. Don't they know there is no such thing as a coincidence? If they took the time to dissect some of the unexplainable events that occur in their lives, they'd realize there is always a greater power in play," she says.

"I know. How insane is it that *Chuy* entrusted *us* to be the ones to convince our loved ones this is all legit? *And* we get to inspire a fairy-tale love story in the process."

"I could not feel *more* privileged to have this distinguished honor."

"Me, too. Beyond grateful." I pause. "Now, let's go support Finn and watch him *crush* this show."

"Deal."

#

We watch as Mac escorts Finn to the brownstone in Brooklyn where filming will take place. It's phenomenal. The grand walk-up entrance is laid out with a curved staircase lined with intricate, metal gates. It's an open concept floor plan with lofted twelve-foot coffered ceilings and a wall of windows overlooking the small but luxurious garden. It has four floors, eight bedrooms on two different levels, eight bathrooms, and two kitchens. The furnishings are nothing short of exquisite.

The Cuisine Network, sponsoring the show, owns the property. They plan to host out of town actors on local projects when the *Delectable* taping is over. They partnered with the Home Network to design the space. Cameras are everywhere. Contestants begin to arrive one by one. There are eight men and eight women in total from all over the United States, ranging from Boston to Texas and of all ages. Some of them have formal training; others claim to be self-taught, and two are specialized pastry chefs.

Finn is a combination of both. He's self-taught, has formal training, and his most recent position was head chef in Paris. In walks a cowboy, decked out in a five-gallon hat, jeans, a huge belt buckle, and cowboy boots. He's about six feet two, brown hair, and has a big beer belly. His name is Jimmy Bolt. He lives on a ranch in Dripping Springs, Texas. It's a small town just outside of Austin, Texas.

"He seems like a cheerful guy," I observe.

"Yes, he's a key part of Finn's journey," Frank says.

"Oh yeah, how so?"

"Well, he's a wholesome cowboy with a tremendous heart. He'll keep Finn grounded. He also went through a tragic loss. He lost his twin brother in a farming accident. It was three days before 9/11."

"Wow, that's horrible."

"Indeed. Jimmy's never left Texas, until now, so in a way they're both branching out of their comfort zone for the first time. He's running from grief, too. You know men grieve differently than women. They attempt to escape their grief by changing scenery or immersing themselves in chaos, hoping to block out the pain. Finn's background is in international cuisine. Jimmy will be the perfect complement as his specialty is BBQ and Tex-Mex — which, by the way, is his new nickname."

"You know I love a good nickname," I quip.

"He and Finn, combined, are a force to be reckoned with. The playful pressure will require Finn to up his game. Tex exposes him to new techniques and combinations. They are both competitors, so they strive for the best but learn from each other and in the process become good friends. Finn's going to win this entire contest by a mere fraction. Tex will be right on his heels. They confide in to each other and realize they are better as a team than individuals. Tex will follow Finn to Vegas where they ride out their year working at Mint. Then, when Finn decides to invest his winnings to open a restaurant of his own, Tex invests with him. They research for locations throughout the west but land on Palm Springs. They work with a commercial realtor and open Christine's. They're both loners, in a sense, but together they create an underlying foundation. Neither of them feels at home anywhere, so they unknowingly create one. Once their settled and life starts to take over, they expand back to Tex's roots in Austin."

". . . which is where Hank's life is pulling her. So, he is a key piece to this puzzle."

"It's amazing to watch him in action. The focus. I've always told him to use his hands, that's his natural born gift." She pauses. "Wait, *that's it*. The journal. . . it's called *The Gift*. That is my mission. I need to convince Finn to stay true to his calling and always use his hands. He can pour his heart out into every dish he makes. I couldn't be prouder of him. His driving force is keeping my legacy alive. The restaurant will be what saves him. Once he feels established, he'll be open and ready to start his life over."

"It's great that he can follow a defined path back to healing, whether he realizes it or not. Hank's . . . a hot mess!"

#

ENTRY #3

My beloved Hank,

The plan is in motion. I hate to say it, but things are about to get much worse before they get better. For that, I'm sorry but the reason is because that's the only way for me to get through to you. I must break you down to the point where your only option is to explode out of the mold that has you trapped. I can't risk you getting comfortable. I know you. You'll settle for mediocrity, complacency and being average. You're not meant to settle. You're meant to follow your dreams and soar. That's when everything comes together for you. I promise it's well worth the wait.

Anyway, more soon.

I love you forever and always,

Danny

CHAPTER SEVEN

"Pull up a chair. Are you sure you're ready for this shit show?"

"Poor Hank. I feel bad she's struggling so much, but this is the catalyst to her life changing forever."

"I'm so proud of her, too. She has real gumption — in a way I never witnessed until I got here. She's never been truly tested until now. I guess you never know how you'll react until you're in the situation. She's handling all her duties this like a champ. I let her fight any of my battles any day. She will always persevere. She's never down too long. It's the fuel that propels her forward. She gets fiery and takes no prisoners. I love that about her. She demonstrates pure strength. She's a warrior," I say.

"What's the back story here?" Frank asks.

"Things started out well at the job. She's leading one of the critical technical system implementations — The Patient Portal, where patients can log into a website to see their test results, consult with their medical team, and receive support from other patients going through similar treatment. A few months into the role, the cracks started to appear in this "perfect" company. The head honcho, Doug Hemsworth, also known as the *Class A Douchebag*, is a tyrant. He has zero interpersonal skills and leads with an iron fist. Pretty contradictory considering Hellyxia is trying to help heal and cure people with their product, Brcaxia."

"Oh, yeah, the Hellyxia Executive Team has dinner at Christine's when they are out in Palm Springs for a Product Launch. Finn kicks him out for berating one of his employees. Then he goes off on Doug for not helping me by giving me the clinical trial. As a consolation, they donate fifty thousand dollars in my name to the Susan G. Komen Foundation," Frank says.

"Yes, that's the one. He puts stress, anxiety and fear into his employees. Everyone walks on egg shells around him. It's a horrible culture. Things weren't adding up for Hank, so she did a little digging into Doug and found herself a golden ticket. She put pieces of the puzzle together that Doug is not who he says he is. She's been concealing this secret to use as leverage when the time comes. Well, the moment is now. . . " I say, as we settle ourselves into the conference room to watch Hank in her element.

#

Hank is on her way to her executive status update with the board. Each month, the board arranges a status update meeting with the directors on all the critical technology projects in progress. She has thirty minutes to provide a demo of her current project, the Patient Portal, and walk through the pilot launch strategy and timeline, which is deploying in four weeks. The meeting commences. She's up first on the agenda. Just as she is about to take the stage, Doug stands up and says, "I'm not comfortable with the progress of Olivia's efforts, so I'm putting this project on hold."

"Look at her face. Her blood is boiling," I say to Frank.

"Excuse me, Doug? I'm a little taken back. I have a presentation prepared that demonstrates the project status is green. We have minimal bugs and are more than prepared for go live."

"It's been brought to my attention that you've been absent several days over the past week, so I'm not confident we've had the proper oversight. This is one of our most important projects. We can't take any chances, so I'm proposing to hand this over to Chris Peters. He is more than equipped to see this through to execution. I need a few additional weeks, so he can get up to speed."

"Where was she and who is Chris Peters?" Frank asks.

"She was out sick but working remotely, so this is a ploy for Doug to undermine her. Chris Peters is his pathetic sidekick. Chris has his head so far up Doug's ass that his rotten British teeth are now a lovely light brown color." Frank laughs. "*She is going to lose her shit. . .*"

"Doug, maybe we can take this offline after the meeting, so I can better understand your position," she says.

Doug interrupts, "That won't be necessary; I've made my final decision. You are excused, Olivia."

"Oh no you *didn't. . .*" I say, waving my finger.

"Oh buddy, you better run for your life." Frank cringes.

"Okay, but before I leave, *Doug*, the Executive Leadership Team might be interested to learn that your real name is not Doug Hemsworth. It's Carl Edges. Does that ring a bell?" He looks at her in disbelief. He turns pale white and realizes what she's going to say next will bury him alive.

"You see, it seems Doug Hemsworth was your best friend growing up in Madison, Wisconsin, who died from non-Hodgkin's lymphoma when he was nineteen. He had a very impressive albeit short life. The article I read stated he graduated with multiple degrees, earning him very honorable and elite accreditations from the University of Wisconsin. All I could find on Carl Edges were mug shots from two DUIs and, wouldn't you know it, those mug shots look exactly like you. In addition, he has multiple arrests for misdemeanor battery charges; seems like someone has a bit of an anger management problem, which explains a lot. And the only degree I could find for him was a two-year associates's degree from a community college. The only logical conclusion I could come up with was that you've stolen your friend's identity and heroic credentials to get yourself a fancy little corner office. Isn't it amazing — what you can find on the internet with a little digging?"

The people in the room are aghast.

"Go, Hank, go!" I cheer.

She looks over at Chris Peters, who looks like he's about to vomit, and adds in a British accent, "I didn't even bother looking you up. You're pretty self-explanatory."

It's evident that Doug has no words. He fumbles to discredit her but to no avail.

"So, my parting words to you and your fake friend, Petey, are . . . go fuck yourselves."

"*Boom!* That's my girl," I say.

And with that, Hank reaches in her purse, grabs an external hard drive, and hands it to the CEO.

"I've saved you the trouble and provided all the proof you need right here. In case you think you can bury this to save the company from a very public and humiliating scandal, I've made multiple copies. Those copies are with my lawyer," she says as she storms out. She gets in her car and heads straight for the airport. She's getting on the next flight to Garrett's. She not even bothering to tell him she's coming. Next stop Palm Springs. She has an emergency gym bag tucked away in her trunk for this purpose.

"Wait for it, Hank, here it comes. . ." I say.

She pulls up to the stop light, still in shock from the events that just went down. Staring her dead in the face is a license plate that reads *Hank* and she burst into tears.

"These are the hardest moments. Not being able to comfort her and reassure her that this is all happening for a reason. The *best* reason," Franks adds as Hank begs and pleads with me for answers.

Danny, I wish you could just tell me what the plan is because nothing is adding up. You keep giving me these signs, but the puzzle isn't fitting together. I am soooo tired of waiting, and I don't even know what I'm waiting for. For something good to happen, for starters. I know there isn't any magical destination, but there must be something more, something bigger. I thought it was this job. The greater purpose. Helping women overcome cancer. Leveraging my talents to connect, heal, and inspire others. Instead, it ended up with my career imploding. I'll be lucky to even get a job after this. Ugh, what am I going to do? You need to help me, now. I'm not messing around anymore. I mean, the company had the word Hell in it. How could I be so stupid? Is there even a Beyond to believe in? Can you even hear me? I'm exhausted. My faith continues to be tested. I mean, am I really making life-changing decisions based on songs that I just happen to hear on the radio?"

"Ummmm, first, yes, because that is what you asked me to send you. Second, I'm *right* here! I've got you! I'll *always* have you. I promise. This is not the end, it's *just* the beginning. *Please* trust me," I scream.

After an exhausting day, she arrives in Palm Springs and climbs into the Uber. She gives the driver Garrett's address when "Small Town" comes on the radio.

"*Really*, Danny? Nice try. What does that even mean? Oh, I'm supposed to be in this Uber right now? Not buying it, sorry."

"Oh boy, you have a lot of work to do," Frank says.

"Tell me about it." I hang my head in my hands. "How long is eternity again?"

#

"This is going to be fun. Let the games begin." Frank watches Hank explain her unplanned arrival to Garrett.

"It's about time. That place seemed shady from day one. You can stay here as long as you need to. Does anyone know you're here?"

"No, I pulled out of the parking lot at work, went straight to the airport, and got on the next plane."

"Is anyone going to be worried about you?"

"No, I was supposed to be leaving for a conference for the week tonight, so everyone thinks I'm out of town, anyway."

"Good. No more excuses about why you might not make it out here for the grand opening of Gin & Tonic. I could really use your help," Garrett says.

"This is her first time at Garrett's new house. His primary home is in Dana Point, California. His original store there is called Cotton, where he sells his own bedding and accessory line. He's a well-known celebrity designer. He's done several of the *Real Housewives'* homes and has made quite a name for himself. He decided to expand up to Palm Springs. This is a huge weekend get away destination for the elite. Perfect strategy on his part. Finn didn't even realize when he opened Christine's what a gold mine he tapped into."

"That's the thing. He leads with his heart. He laid down roots where it feels right," Frank says as we see Hank stirring. . .

#

She awakens to the sun glaring in her face. The house is so new; he doesn't have any window treatments. Right now, she's finding it more aggravating than amusing, seeing as her cousin owns a store that specializes in this exact thing — blinds. She forces herself out of bed to take in mountains as far as the eye can see. Her bedroom has a sliding glass door with direct access onto the patio, which is a stunning desert oasis. Very private, fenced-in yard with a beautiful pool and adjacent hot tub. The built- in waterfall is so soothing to listen to. She steps outside to breathe in the crisp desert air. Garrett and Tristan are both already well into their day, so she decides to take a morning soak in the hot tub. The yard is secluded enough so she goes au natural. She keeps replaying yesterday's events, wishing there was someone to bring her endless mimosas to dull the pain when she is jolted back to reality.

"Hello? Hello . . . . *Olivia?*"

"Sweet Jesus. Who is here? I'm naked and it's daytime," Hank grumbles. There isn't an ounce of clothing within arm's length *or* a towel.

"You're mean. You're having their first meet be when she is most vulnerable? She's *naked!*"

"Maybe this will teach her to start listening to me. Then I wouldn't have to go to such extremes to make a point. I mean, come on. It hasn't even been twenty-four hours since her life crumbled into a million pieces, and I'm serving up the man of her dreams," I respond.

"And I guess Garrett failed to mention he had a handsome, five-star chef coming over this morning to provide a sample tasting menu for his upcoming grand opening of Gin & Tonic?" she asks.

"Conveniently. . . "

Finn tries knocking on the front door. Garrett texted and said Olivia would be at the house waiting for him, so when Finn doesn't get an answer, he proceeds over to the rear gate to see if he can find her.

"Hello? Olivia . . . are you back here?"

"Ummmmmmmmm, yes, but I'm in the hot tub and, ummmmmm, I don't have any clothes on . . . or a towel." She scrambles when she sees him turn the corner.

"They'll laugh at this someday," I say.

"I'd *kill* you," Frank says.

"Oh my God, I'm so sorry. I'll give ye a second and meet ye at the front door," Finn says.

"Okay, thanks," Hank yells. It's funny watching her scramble. She is *freaking* out.

"Um . . . hi, I'm Olivia, Garrett's cousin." She drinks him in from head to toe. All six feet two of him with his sandy brown hair, baby blue eyes, and athletic build.

"Aww, it's so cute. Look how nervous he is," Frank says. "It's perfect; you caught him off guard. He doesn't even know what hit him."

"Just wait until she gets another earful of that Scottish accent. She's done for."

"And so it *begins...* " Frank swoons.

Hank and Finn have a flirty day of menu tasting, but he's trying to keep it professional since Garrett hired him as the caterer. He doesn't want to mix business and pleasure.

\#

ENTRY #4

> *My beloved Hank,*
>
> *Well, it happened! YOU DID IT!!!!! You quit that horrible job and it was EPIC! You walked away from what you thought was safety, security, and a life of substance. You threw caution to the wind and came out fighting. I'm so, SO proud of you! This is such a valuable lesson. The first of many. You're learning to listen to your intuition. You're acting on it, without hesitation, regardless of the circumstances. Your instincts are in line with the universe and although you can't put all the pieces of the puzzle together just yet, this was a GIANT step in the right direction.*
>
> *I know you know I'm here, even through all the doubt, fear, and tears. The road ahead is going to be a bit bumpy, but you can handle it. You're WAY*

stronger than you give yourself credit for. Your spunk, courage, bravery, and tenacity are going to get you there. No matter how small the step, keep moving forward. You got over the first HUGE hurdle. You jumped off the cliff without a safety net.

This decision is going to lead you to incredible things, namely, one Mr. Finn McDaniels, who I've personally handpicked for you. He's the love of your life. He's charming, generous, thoughtful, and compassionate. His passion for cooking is going to inspire you to find your purpose. He's going to be the first person you will open your heart up to because he feels like home to you. I couldn't ask for a better man to love you. He will take care of your heart and soul.

Anyway, more soon.

I love you forever and always,

Danny

CHAPTER EIGHT

Today is the grand opening of Gin & Tonic. Hank arrives at five-thirty with Garrett and Tristan to help set up before the guests arrive at seven. She steps into the kitchen to say hello, in her fitted black and white cocktail dress with red patent leather sling-backs, when Finn catches a glimpse of her.

"Aye, Olivia. Ye look smashing," he says.

"Look at how adorable he is. He's like a giddy school boy. I wish I could go back and see his reaction to our first meeting," Frank says.

"I won't lie. It is cute to see how enamored he is with her," I say.

"Thank you. Anything I can help with?" she asks.

"It's funny to watch her flirt. She's pretending to be helpful but really just wants to get a reaction out of him," I say.

"Mission accomplished. Look at him watching her saunter about. I do believe she's sparked a flame that's been extinguished for quite some time," she says.

The invite list includes three hundred of the most prestigious people in Palm Springs. It's great exposure for *both* Garrett and Finn. Crowds begin to arrive, and the space is bubbling with conversation and laughter. Each guest is greeted with the signature Gin & Tonic cocktail of the evening by hot, young waiters and waitresses. Garrett is hoping to sell several of the pieces he is showcasing tonight, so the traffic flow is set up. Hank works her charm and mingles with the crowd.

The party livens up around ten after the drinks have been flowing. The DJ sets things into full motion.

Hank is still unsteady from the events of the last several days, so she's sampling every drink within arms reach to try to numb her pain. As things are winding down, she sees Finn cleaning up the last of the dessert table. Their eyes lock from across the room, and he gives her a smile with a wink.

"It doesn't take much to melt her heart," I say. "But *wait for i. . .*"

"Can I help you with those?" Hank says, approaching Finn to help him with the rest of his clean up. She grabs a couple of serving platters and follows him outside to his truck. Just as he sets down his cart, I see her losing her balance. Next thing you know, she's flat on her ass and his platters are airborne.

"*Daniel. . .* that is *not* funny. Did you just push her???" Frank scolds.

"Oh *shit!*" I laugh. "*Chuy* said I wouldn't have those powers, but you know me, I had to test it anyway. I didn't think it would work."

"Good thing Finn is a gentleman and will think it's adorable," Frank says, "but you are in *soooo* much trouble with *Chuy*."

"I swear, I didn't think it would work." I am unable to control my laughter.

"Are ye gonna be all right there, lassie?" Finn asks. "I can't tell if yer laughing or crying."

Hank is laughing uncontrollably but manages to give him the international thumbs up sign for a-okay.

"*See? She* thinks it's funny, too. Instant classic move."

"I hate to laugh, but as long as yer all right I have to say that was the fanciest wipe out I've ever seen. I don't even think ye had time to brace yourself. Here, let me help ye up." Just as she stabilizes, he looks at her with the sweetest concerned face.

"Ye sure yer okay?" he asks again as she gets a little liquid courage and goes in for a kiss. He lingers for a sweet moment then pulls away.

"Olivia, um, I think ye've had too much to drink. Yer bloody fantastic, but ye should know . . ." Before he finishes the sentence, she can sense the shift in his demeanor. She's made him uncomfortable and rejection settles in.

"Right, no . . . no, I'm *so* sorry. Thanks again for everything. I'll have Garrett follow up with you tomorrow. Have a good night." She turns on her heel to run back into the store as fast as she can. She hides behind the cash wrap, humiliated.

"Oh no, she misread him. He's interested. He was just caught off-guard," Franks says.

Really, Danny? Is anything ever going to go my way, or are you determined to watch me make an ass out of myself for the rest of my life? He's gay. What am I doing?

Frank and I dissolve into hysterics realizing Hank thinks Finn's gay.

"Poor thing," Frank says.

"And by that you mean poor Finn, right? He's got some *splaining* to do."

Christine, you need to help me; you know I'm not good at this. When I met you, it was like you appeared from nowhere; I guess it's not too dissimilar to how I met Olivia, but I don't know how to pursue someone. I'm out of my league here. If I am meant to pursue this, give me another shot, present me with another opportunity.

"You've totally got this, babe. Don't sweat it. I'm here and won't let you stumble," Frank says.

#

Hank is just emerging from her two-day hangover at Garrett's when she realizes she can't avoid the elephant in the room any longer. She decides she needs to face Finn and apologize for being so forward. She gets cleaned up and drives to the restaurant to see if she can catch him. She spots a car parked in the alley behind the restaurant. It's a small, black Mercedes convertible with a vanity plate inscribed *Danny Boy*.

Really, Danny? As if allowing me to kiss a gay man weren't enough, now the license plate? You're killing me.

She musters up the courage to knock on the door, all the while her inner voice convincing herself that not knowing he's gay is an honest mistake. When he opens the door, she is overcome with the scent of garlic, chocolate, and sweaty man.

"Olivia, hi. What a pleasant surprise. Please, please come in," Finn greets, inviting her into the kitchen.

"I'll try not to trip and break anything this time," she jokes.

"I was wondering how you were feeling. I meant to call yesterday. . . "

"Listen, Finn, I came to apologize for my behavior the other night. I'm mortified I crossed the line. I don't know what came over me. Then to realize you don't even like women makes it that much more humiliating."

"Ummm, what?" he asks.

"Okay, I'm not going to lie, this is pretty hilarious watching him squirm, being forced to explain his sexual preference," Frank adds.

"I understand if it's not something you're comfortable talking about, but, so you know, some of

76

my best friends are gay. I've just never hit on them before because I have good gaydar."

Just as Hank is finishing her sentence, she collapses. Finn grabs a cold towel and places it on her forehead. As she comes to, he hands her a glass of ice water.

"That was ALL her, I swear. I had nothing to do with that one. That's pure dehydration," I say.

"Ye gonna be all right there, lass? Sit here." Finn extends his hand to help her up.

"I have to stop falling and breaking things around you." She laughs.

"Can I get you something? Have you eaten?"

"I'm still so hungover from Saturday night, I haven't eaten anything since . . . well, your chocolate fountain."

"Lucky for ye, yer in a restaurant. Let me make something real quick." She's mesmerized watching him in his element. He moves about the kitchen so effortlessly and, to top it off, he's in his everyday clothes so the rough and gruff package is releasing some serious pheromones. As he whips up homemade lobster mac and cheese, he explains the license plate is a tribute to his mom. She always wanted to name him Daniel, but his last name is McDaniels, so that wasn't going to work. She called him Danny anyway.

"Here ye go. Hangover comfort food at its best."

She inhales every morsel. "Wow, this might be the best food that has ever crossed these lips."

"Glad you enjoyed it. Why don't ye come back tomorrow night after close, when yer feeling better, and we'll make dinner together?"

"A fresh start, I'd like that. Listen, I really am . . ."

Before she can finish her sentence, he grabs her by the waist and pulls her toward him, one hand on her lower back and the other making its way to her chin. He gives her a slow, sweet and passionate kiss. Still feeling woozy from fainting, she opens her eyes to ensure she's not still in bed, dreaming. When she meets his eyes, he declares with a huge smile, "By the way, I'm not gay. I'm a widower. See you tomorrow night."

#

I hear the *Mission Impossible* song playing on repeat in my head as Hank is on a quest to fluff and buff herself before her big date tonight with Finn. As she leaves her final stop, the hair salon, she catches the light of a neon sign across the parking lot that says *Psychic Readings by Kelly. Walk-Ins Welcome*. It's like a magnetic pull. She can't ignore it. I know she's scared to death. She's already captivated with Finn. She wants reassurance, so she can let her guard down. She doesn't want to invest and open herself up to getting hurt. As much as she wants to believe, she is the biggest skeptic at heart. Doubt is always lurking. That, and she's the most impatient human on the planet. She's lucky I love her so much. I guarantee *anyone* else would have thrown in the towel by now.

"Here we go. This is the big break we've been waiting for. She's finally taking the leap," I say to Frank as Hank takes a deep breath and enters. *Dan, let's do this.*

A friendly woman in her mid-forties with short blondish hair and a beautiful and inviting smile welcomes her.

"Please, come in. Don't be nervous. Is this your first time?"

"Yes,"

"Make yourself comfortable. Don't worry, this isn't any sort of voodoo or witchcraft. I've been doing this for a long time. My name is Kelly."

"Hi, Kelly, my name is Olivia."

"Pleasure to meet you, Olivia," she says, extending her hand to lead Hank to the back room where she will conduct the reading. It's a small but cozy room. It has two giant, white, fluffy chairs. Not to be cheesy but they almost look like clouds. The chairs sit in front of a modern fireplace. The mantle is strewn with white, lit candles of all different shapes and sizes. The ceiling has a series of strung lights, made to look like stars, covered with delicate white tulle. The candles and ceiling lights are the only things lighting the space, which make it a very inviting, calming, and warm place. She gestures for Hank to have a seat in the first chair.

"I tried to ignore spirit for a long time myself but they are very persistent. Once I gave in, I learned to embrace it as a gift. I consider it a gift because I can connect loved ones here in the physical world with their treasured ones on the other side. How can that not be fulfilling? So, the way I work is I have you sit here for a couple minutes, state three wishes, and ask for one specific thing you would like for your loved one to present to you during the reading to validate it is them. I find that process clears the mind and leaves you more open to receiving whatever messages may be waiting for you."

"Okay." Hank quivers as she closes her eyes and start.

Dan, I'm not going to lie; I'm kind of freaking out. I want nothing more than to connect with you. Please, please, please, come through. If you are here, say something about our musical connection or have her mention Chuck Taylors. Then I will know.

My three wishes are:

1. *To meet a wonderful, compassionate, generous, loving man who is my ultimate soulmate; who will cherish me, our connection, and who will promise to love me forever. Oh, and he has to be funny — that is an absolute must. Annnnnnnd while we're at it, throw in handsome. Sorry, one last thing — a chef would be amazing.*

2. *My second wish is to find my purpose and passion in life. Why am I here? What have I been put on this earth to do? Help me find it, be successful at it, and I want it to be rewarding. Heal my soul kind of rewarding.*

3. *My last wish is for the people I love most. Please protect them and watch over them; keep them safe, happy, and healthy, always. You know who they are.*

"I'm here, Hank. You don't need an interpreter, silly. I hear every request, every plea, every prayer. What I want more than anything is for you to know that I will protect your heart forever, for eternity. I won't let anyone hurt you. I brought you here so now you need to leave it in my hands. I wouldn't place Finn into your life and not follow through. I know the hardship you carry. I want only the best for you, so you can heal and live the life you're meant to live. I'm begging you to stop worrying and surrender to it."

"Okay, I'm ready," she says to Kelly.

"Let's get started." She closes her eyes and places her hands over Hank's while whispering a prayer. "Spirit, please protect Olivia and guide her with your love and light, in all things good, always and forever. Amen."

"Amen."

"Hellllllllllllloooooooooo, can you see me?" I say, doing jumping jacks trying to get Kelly's attention.

"Wow, right away I have someone here that is eager to get through. A young male in his early twenties. Do you know who this would be?"

"Yes."

"Please tell her how *sorry* I am. I was shocked when I got here, too. I couldn't believe it! It happened in a split second. Please tell her I'm so sorry for the pain I've caused everyone and to send my love to my family. It's so hard for me to know how much grief they're in." I wave a handkerchief so she gets the "Hanky" reference.

"He keeps saying I'm so sorry, I'm so sorry. He said his passing was sudden, tragic, and unexpected. Is that true?"

"Uh huh," Hank responds.

"He says no one was more surprised with his passing than he was. That in the blink of an eye, he was just gone and on the other side. It happened in an instant. He knows the sadness and pain his passing has caused for his family and you. I am seeing the name Hank; was that his name?"

I can see Hank's body break out with goosebumps. She's so stunned, she can barely get the words out.

"*Seeeeee,* I told you I'm here."

81

"Wow, this is incredible. Unbelievable. No, that was his nickname for me," she says, welling up with tears.

"Oh, no, *please don't cry* . . . Don't you see how amazing this is . . . we're talking. Don't be sad," I say.

"That is him validating he's here. He has a great deal of love for you and knows how often you talk to him. He said he sends you songs and license plates. Those are not coincidences."

"I can't believe this," Hank responds.

"Okay, Frank you're up. Let's see if she can put this together. . . " I say.

"Hi Liv, it's Frank. You don't know it yet but I'm here with Danny. . . we're conspiring to bring you and Finn together. It's meant to be . . . trust us."

"Okay, now there is a woman coming through. About the same age. She died of an illness. It left and came back. I'm feeling something in my chest and abdomen. Do you know who this is?"

"No, I don't know who that would be. I don't know anyone else young who has passed," Hank says.

"She and your friend know each other, and they want you to know they are together on the other side," Kelly says.

"That's really odd. I have no idea who that would be, but I'm glad he has a companion. Maybe he's introducing me to his girlfriend. I wouldn't be surprised if that was the first thing he did when he got there. He was quite the ladies' man."

"*Heeeeeyyyyyyyy now*. Easy there. She's not my girlfriend. It's just Frank. I'm trying to work on finding one, but someone has me a *little* pre-occupied." I roll my eyes then slam the door.

"He's really funny. He's clowning around. They have their arms interlocked, almost like they are squaredancing, and can't stop giggling. Was he funny?" Kelly asks.

"Only the funniest person I've ever met."

"He's showing me a door. That symbolizes an ending. Did you end something?"

"Yes, I just quit my job."

"Okay, he says there's a huge shift coming in your life. He wants you to know how protective he is of you, so you need to trust him. You will be able to leave the pain in the past and move on. He assures me they will always be with you. He also said you will be moving in the next six months. Does that make sense?"

"Wow, I hope so."

As Kelly ends the session, she asks, "Was it what you were hoping for? What you expected?"

"I'm so overwhelmed and grateful. You truly are amazing. You have a tremendous gift. I can'tbelieve he mentioned Hank. Mind blowing. I asked him for a different sign, but it would be just like him to do it his way. He was always so thoughtful. He loved to plan surprises. Like the take your breath away bombshells. You have no idea how much peace and comfort this gives me. Knowing he can hear me. That he's always with me. I will make sure to tell his family, too. Very healing. Thank you." She leans over to hug Kelly goodbye. She closes her eyes and imagines the hug is from me even though nothing could ever measure up.

"You're welcome, Hank," I say. "I wish there was a way I could send her Whitney Houston's, 'I Will Always Love You.' I think she'd get it."

"Awww, that's so sweet. You literally blew her mind."

"That should cover her until at least noon tomorrow," I say and we both laugh.

#

ENTRY #5

My beloved Hank,

Do you believe me now? Tonight's your first date with Finn and you had a reading with Kelly who flawlessly interpreted my entire message. She's good. How can you question that? How could she possibly know 1) I'm a guy . . . okay, I guess she had a fifty/fifty chance there but 2) how would she know I was in my mid-twenties 3) I mean, the Hank thing? Come on. Really?! I love you, Hank, but please use some common sense here. If you think logically, you will know there is absolutely no logical explanation for what just happened. We communicated. You can try to ignore it as much as you want but there is no denying it. We are deeply connected. Also, do you really think I'm going to hand deliver everything you've prayed for in a man only to rip it away from you? After everything? Feel it in your soul, the deep love . . . the energy. Let it grow. How could he possibly not fall in love with you? You're the best there is.

Anyway, more soon.

I love you forever and always,

Danny

CHAPTER NINE

We arrive to the restaurant at five o'clock for the big night.

"How's Finn holding up?" I ask Frank as we watch Finn prepare for their first date.

"He's a nervous wreck. It's adorable. He called Jules to get advice. As much as he didn't want to reveal the reason was a girl, he was desperate. Now, Tex is getting in on the fun, making kissy faces, teasing him about his date. It's been a long time since he's put himself out there. Our connection happened so naturally, he didn't really need to pursue me," she says.

"Ah, he's got plenty of game. Plus, she'll fall instantly in love with his charm. They are going to fall in love without any effort. They need to trust it." I see Hank pull up. Finn seeks the last bit of encouragement from Frank.

Okay, Christine, here goes nothing. Remember . . . show me a sign.

"This is perfect because Hank is wearing the claddagh necklace you gave her for graduation. He will recognize it right away," Frank says.

"He's going to stop dead in his tracks, watch."

Finn greets her at the back door with a glass of prosecco. As he leans in to give her a kiss, he's paralyzed. He gets an eyeful of Hank's claddagh necklace, the one matching Christine's, and is stunned.

"Hi . . . is everything okay? You have a startled look on your face," Hank says with hesitation.

"Yes, yes, of course. You look smashing. Lovely necklace. Please, please come in."

"Thank you. I could certainly get used to being greeted with a glass of prosecco wherever I arrive, and the necklace is my most treasured possession, so kind of you to notice." She grabs the charm. Finn is still shaken from seeing the necklace and tries to pull it together. He's not ready to talk about Christine. He doesn't want the conversation to get too heavy. He wants to keep this night light and fun. He starts with a tour of the restaurant.

"This is spectacular. I love the décor, very Roaring Twenties, classy. And the name, Christine's, I presume, is named after your late wife."

"Yes," he responds. "Garrett certainly hit it out of the park with the design. Couldn't be more pleased with it."

As they prepare dinner, Finn fills her in on his *Delectable* journey.

"Vegas was too much for me. When the search began, my requirements were warm, sunny, within three to four hours of the beach and a major city, active lifestyle, and a city with a clientele willing to frequent an upper tier restaurant. As soon as I saw this place, I knew this was it."

"Well done. I commend you for pursuing your dream. Not many people have the guts to go for it. I'm kind of a workaholic."

"This hasn't been easy," he acknowledges. "So, why are you out here in Palm Springs? Just visiting?"

"I had planned on coming out for Garrett's big opening but decided to come out a little early because uh, I, uh, quit my job and not just quit; I kind of blew up the island."

"Really? What happened?"

"To make a long story short, let's say I thought I was working at an amazing, cutting-edge company only to find out that one of the officers was a complete fraud. He used fake credentials to land his position, proceeded to make hundreds of people's lives miserable, and I exposed him during an executive meeting. Someday, I'll share the specifics with you, but since you don't know me that well, I don't want you to think I'm some crazy drama queen."

"To be a fly on that wall," he comments. They continue getting to know each other as he prepares filet and crab legs. He has a table set with a beautiful bouquet of flowers.

"I've been meaning to tell you:your accent is dreamy. I'm sure that's part of the allure for all the ladies."

"Aye, right."

"Tell me about your family."

"I grew up in a small town. . . " Suddenly, Hank starts coughing, triggered by the mere mention of those weighted words.

"Are ye okay? Here. Drink some water."

"Yes, yes I'm okay. I'm quite the refined lady. I keep tripping in front of you and now I'm coughing up a lung. I bet you can't wait to take me to tea. So classy."

"Nah, stop it. I think it's endearing. It adds to yer charm," he says as she blushes.

"You were saying?" He shares details about his life growing up in St. Andrew's, Scotland.

"My best friend, Mac. I have probably mentioned him? Maybe?"

"No, I don't think so."

"He's my best bloke. He's the brother I never had. He lived four houses down. Inseparable. Both athletic. We golfed, played tennis, rugby, or as you Americans call it, football. And, of course, got into our fair share of shenanigans. Mac is also the funniest person I know."

"There is nothing better than funny. I had a friend just like it," she chimes in.

"Yeah, he lives in Los Angeles now with his wife, Jules, who is another close friend. Mac moved over to New York City as I was entering culinary school. He was chosen to be part of some traveling comedy group and is now in Los Angeles writing his own sitcom."

"Wait. Mac as in Malcolm *Hill?*" she says, baffled.

"Seeeeeeee, I *told you* that you would regret this decision." I turn to Frank. "But she's going to be mad at ME like *I* had something to do with this."

"Yes. You know of him?" Finn asks.

"Um, yeah . . . yeah . . . I . . . uh, took some writing classes at Second City in Chicago and he was a guest instructor for a day, so our paths crossed. He seems like a great guy," she stutters.

"I should ask him if he remembers you; how ironic is that?"

"Oh no, no, he definitely would not remember me. I can guarantee he has no clue who I am. I mean, I only encountered him in passing. I knew who he was because he's considered a god in the Second City community," she says, her voice shifting as she squirms a bit in her chair. "Can you please excuse me for a second?" She stands to excuse herself to the ladies' room.

"Is everything okay? You seem nervous suddenly." He pleads with Frank as Hank smiles and walks away.

Christine, you need to help me here. I don't have any game. Am I putting her off? The mood suddenly shifted. I'm not sure if it's something I said? Please, help. I don't want this to go south.

She returns, and they spend the next several hours telling story after story, laughing and falling in love.

#

Hank gets into her car and lays into me.

How could you? How could you do this to me? Send me straight into the eye of the storm? Meet the ONE person that has a connection with the stupidest decision in my life? My one-night stand? And not only a connection but they are best friends, like brothers, like us. This is unforgivable. Finn will never forgive Mac or ever want to be with me if he finds out. And hello? You not only arranged, plotted or planned . . . or whatever it is you're doing up there, but I'm pretty sure I am already falling in love with him. WHY? Why are you doing this to me? Is this some practical joke from the other side? I DO NOT think it's funny. What am I going to do? This is a disaster. You and I are officially in a fight. I mean it. Silent treatment level. You're on notice, mister.

"Can you please help me understand how this is *my* fault?" I ask Frank, shaking my head.

"Give her a break. She's terrified. She's already lost control of her heart and she knows it. There's no turning back now. She's done for."

"It's not that big of a deal. She needs to let go of the past."

"Easier for you to say. The wound is still wide open."

"Maybe Garrett will talk some sense into her."

She's crying as she bursts into the house, screaming "GARREEETTTTT."

"Jesus, sweetie. What is it? Are you okay?" he asks, alarmed.

"I can't believe this is happening," she blubbers. "This is the shit that only happens to me."

"What happened? Did he do something to you?"

"No, no. Oh my God . . . no. Okay, you ready for it? Remember a couple of years ago when I had that one-night stand? The one with that hot Scottish instructor from my Second City class?"

"Yeah, what about it?"

"He's Finn's best fucking friend from home."

"Well, ain't that a pisser."

"Don't joke. It's not funny. What am I going to do? I can't start a relationship with him knowing I slept with his best friend. The one guy he considers his brother no less. Oh, and to top it off, he probably thinks I have explosive diarrhea because I excused myself from the table a couple of times to go to the bathroom to have a meltdown."

"Why didn't you text me?"

"My phone was in my purse across the room. It would've been too obvious," she squeals, pacing back and forth in the kitchen.

"Sweetie, take a deep breath. It's going to be fine."

"How?"

"You said it was a few years ago, right?"

"Yeah. Finn mentioned Mac is married now."

"And you were both drunk, right?"

"Well yes, I don't remember any of it — going to the hotel, the sex, none of it."

"How did you leave it? Did you exchange numbers, last names?"

"No, I woke up, freaked out and ran out as fast as I could. I never even went back to class."

"It's fine. He's a *guy*. A straight man. He doesn't remember. Trust me."

"No, she wishes he didn't remember . . . he remembers," I add.

"Great, now you're making me feel like a slut," she responds, deflated.

"No. That's not what I mean. He's probably a player. Hooked up all the time. You were just another conquest. Forget about it. Seriously," Garrett says.

"I feel so much better. Not. Seriously, you don't think I should tell Finn?"

"Hell no. Take that to the grave. Never mention it again. Not to Red. Not to Jane. I mean it, no one."

"Dude, that's not *entirely* realistic but she does need to put it aside for now, so they can continue building their relationship. It's not insurmountable," I say.

"Yes, their date tonight is *critical*. It's the no turning back moment between them. If she says something now, she'll ruin it and they'll never get there. *Damn free will,*" Frank adds.

"I know. That's the hardest part of this job. Not being able to insert ourselves. She's her biggest obstacle."

#

Hank arrives at Finn's house at seven-thirty with a bottle of wine in hand. She's greeted by his adorable rescue golden retriever, Frank.

"Where's Daddy, buddy?" she asks as she spots a glass of wine sitting on the kitchen counter with a note. *Make yourself at home. XO.* She takes a tour while he finishes up in the shower. His home is very Frank Sinatra-esque, old school Palm Springs. The home has a grand, open concept layout with all floor-to-ceiling windows framing the pool. Music is playing. Van Morrison, "Into the Mystic."

"Sorry, I was running late from the restaurant and wanted to get cleaned up."

"I was going to join you in there but decided drowned rat isn't the look I'm going for to kick off the night."

"That would have been fabulous." He leans down to give her a kiss that makes her weak in the knees.

"Now I'm regretting my decision," she says with a giant grin. They make their way into the kitchen. Frank keeps moving around the space, following Finn and plopping down to stay as close to him as he can. He is the cutest.

"How old is Frank?"

"Almost two. After I left the hustle and bustle of Vegas, I figured I should at least have another living being in my house since it can get quiet out here. I love it, though. It's peaceful. I can't deal with crowds or traffic."

"He is the cutest companion you could have."

She's mesmerized watching him work. He's in his zone. Concentrating but making it look so effortless at the same time. He's making shrimp and mushroom risotto. She can tell this is what he was born to do. They eat and get the kitchen cleaned up when Finn excuses himself. He reappears wearing a bathrobe and has another one in his hand for Hank.

"This is all ye'll need for the rest of the night. Go put it on and meet me out in the hot tub."

As she heads to the bedroom to follow her orders, she sees him grab some strawberries, two glasses, and a bottle of champagne. She's welcomed back by soft music streaming through the speakers, a dim lit patio, and a romantic fireplace providing additional warmth to the cold desert air. Finn is already sitting comfortable in the hot bubbles as she approaches.

"Oh no," Frank said. "I feel her pain. There's something about the very first moment a man sees you naked. You don't want it to be full of anxiety, but you start outlining all the flaws in your head and panic."

"Really? Because all we're thinking is how lucky we are that any woman wants to take their clothes off for us, in any situation. At this moment, I guarantee, all he's doing is chanting . . . *please don't change your mind* . . . over and over. Trust me, if we get you this far, it's nothing short of a miracle."

Frank laughs. "That's funny. I had no idea."

"Take it off. I want to drink in every beautiful inch of you," Finn says. "Besides, I've already seen it."

"What? When?"

"The day I met you at Garrett's for the first time. Remember, you were in the hot tub? I took my time making my way to the front door." He grins.

"You *didn't.* I knew it." She takes a deep breath and drops the robe.

"*Oooook*, too much information," I say, turning away. "I'm only here until she tells him about me then when things start getting hot and heavy, I'm gone."

"Don't worry, me too. I don't want to be a voyeur," Frank adds.

Hank gets settled in, and Finn leans in for a sweet kiss while he hands her a glass of champagne. Just as they're getting cozy, Hank's body tenses up when

"Small Town" begins to pipe through his stereo speakers.

"What is it?" he asks.

"It's this song . . . It's nothing. Where were we?" she says, trying to change the subject.

"Tell me," he asks eagerly.

"But I don't want to cry." He puts his hands on her face and looks deeply into her eyes.

"Liv, ye can't scare me. I was drawn to ye the minute I met ye, yer smile, yer wit, yer spirit. Ye exude confidence which makes ye that much more beautiful. I want ye to be raw with me. Just be ye, not some altered version of ye, okay?"

"She's toast," I say.

And with that, the first teardrops fall. She takes a deep breath.

"This song reminds me of my best friend, Dan. He died in a car accident four years ago."

"Oh, Liv. . ."

"He was unbelievable. Truly the best. The only way to describe him is to say he was happiness. He had a smile that could melt any heart, the most contagious laugh you've ever heard, and a giant heart of gold. It was a freak accident." She pauses. "My life changed forever." Tears begin to stream down her face.

"Oh Liv, I am so, so sorry," he says, holding her close to comfort her, and then the fireworks start to fly.

"Annnnnnnnnnnnnnnnnd, I'm out," I say, running for cover.

#

ENTRY #6

My beloved Hank,

We're working our magic up here! The necklace? "Small Town"? I'm dropping missiles left and right, but you'll still wake up tomorrow and wonder if he likes you. I know, I know . . . you're scared. I get it. I really do but it's ME. Who had your back every day of your life from the moment I met you? ME. Nothing has changed. Not. A. Thing. If anything, our friendship is even closer than it was in the physical world. I can see things so much more clearly now. I don't want you to waste time worrying. You need to treasure these moments. They won't last forever. It's my biggest regret. Not living in the moment more. Not loving or laughing harder. It's such a gift. Please don't squander it. We have more to go to get you there, but I'll be here for every ounce of it. I'll hold you through every smile, tear, doubt, and milestone. You're on your way, I promise.

Anyway, more soon.

I love you forever and always,

Danny

CHAPTER TEN

"All I want to do is kiss ye. Do you know how irresistible ye are?" Finn says.

"Aw. I'm enamored with you myself, mister," Hank says. "Is it okay if I ask you about her?"

"About who, Christine? Sure."

"Yes, tell me. I want to know everything about the woman who stole your heart."

"When I was in culinary school in Paris, she spent a year in Europe on a study abroad program. She and I met at the restaurant and became the best of chums. I guess you could say it was a young, whirlwind romance. We were engaged within months. After Christine graduated, we got married right away, and we stayed in Paris to pursue our careers. She was a teacher, and I graduated to head chef at the restaurant, Benoit. After a couple of years, she got pregnant. We were ecstatic. Then about twelve weeks into the pregnancy, our world completely imploded."

"What happened?"

"We thought she was having a miscarriage, so we rushed to the hospital. When they went in to stop the bleeding, her uterus was full of cancer. They performed an immediate hysterectomy. After further tests, they diagnosed her with Stage III breast cancer."

"Oh, Finn. I am so, so sorry," Hank says, wiping tears from her face.

"We were lucky enough to have her in remission for two more years, but then it came back with a vengeance and spread to her bones. She went downhill quickly. We tried to get her into a clinical trial back here in the States, but it was too late."

"I cannot imagine what you've been through. I'm so sorry." She pauses. "The trial wasn't by chance for a drug called Brcaxia, was it?"

"Aye, it was. How do ye know about it?"

"You're not going to believe this, but that's the company I just quit from, or should I say, blew up."

"Yer lyin'! What happened?" She explains the whole story and what led to her boiling point.

"Bloody hell."

"Next thing I remember is standing on Garrett's doorstep."

"Ye won't believe this, but I can add to yer story."

"What do you mean?"

"Hellyxia rented out my restaurant a few months ago for some big product launch. It was a bunch of rich bastarts who thought their shit didn't stink but the ring leader was that Doug fellow."

"No way," she says, aghast.

"I didn't realize who it was until the day before they came in. I saw Hellyxia on the books, and my heart sank. These were the people who couldn't save my wife's life. I mean, what are the chances they would rent out the restaurant dedicated to her? I'm not going to lie; I went into it with such a negative attitude about them and did they ever exceed my expectations. What a bunch of bastarts, Doug in particular. He was ordering my staff around like they were his puppets. He was so blottered he called one of my waitresses a white trash bitch. Thank God, we didn't have any other patrons. The CEO gave us a tremendous tip to make up for their deplorable behavior, but I let them all know they were never welcome again, even individually."

"That is un-fricking-believable. Makes my blood boil. I was supposed to be at that dinner but got out of it. I didn't want to spend time with those idiots. The story sounds exactly like what I just lived through. Outrageous. What ordinary people conduct themselves like that? I am so glad I was the one to take that bastard down, and I'm even happier now, knowing what he did to you. Quitting was the best thing ever."

"So, what's next for you?"

"That's an excellent question. I have no idea. I can say one thing for sure; I am divorced from Corporate America. Never again. I told Garrett I would help at the store for the time being while I try to sort it out. I'm pretending I'm on an extended vacation."

"But I mean, if you could do *anything*? What would you do?"

"That's easy. I'd be a writer. That's always been my dream."

"Intriguing. Continue. What kind of writer?"

"I'm not sure. I love story telling, so I would love to try any of it."

"Maybe Mac can put ye in contact with some of his connections. I mean, my best bloke is a superstar in comedy. He'd be the perfect person for ye to reach out to."

"Uh, yeah, that would be great," she says, changing the subject abruptly. "This might sound like a strange question but do you believe in signs? Like, do you ever talk to Christine and ask her to send you things or help guide you?"

"Aye, only all the time. In fact, before she passed, I asked her to send me things to let me know she was okay. She told me she'd send rainbows and butterflies. Right after her funeral, I was so overwhelmed and inconsolable until a butterfly landed on my shoulder and I just felt like she was at peace."

Through tears she says, "Wow, that is so beautiful. It takes your breath away, doesn't it? Look how far you've come."

"I know. I can't imagine my life any different."

"My signs are songs and license plates for the most part. "Small Town" in particular, which is why I got so emotional last night. Dan and I used to go to concerts together all the time. I picked "Small Town" because the words summed him up. And he always comes through. I still can't believe he's gone."

"I can't believe Christine's gone either."

"Aww, we're right here," Frank says, hugging me.

"I don't tell anyone about it. You understand. I don't want to sound like I've lost it. There are so many skeptics out there. To each his own, but I believe that Dan's still with me, guiding me. I keep a diary of all the things I've asked for and all the answers I've gotten. Some are so crazy I don't want to ever forget them. We fight, too. I get mad at him when he doesn't give me what I want," Hank says with a laugh. "But then he comes through with something ten times better. He's trying to teach me patience, but it's not working very well. I've been trying for years to put all the pieces of this giant puzzle together. The signs were so clear about me taking that job with the pharmaceutical company. I hadn't been able to reconcile why he would send me down such a dark, destructive path full of tension, turmoil, and disappointment . . . until now."

"Until now? How so?"

"He knew me better than anyone. He was aware that my spirit couldn't be contained or controlled. I would never stand for something so unethical and immoral. If I was backed into a corner, he knew I would have to find a way out. It would build like a volcano inside of me, and I would be so miserable I would quit." She paused. "Now I think it's because . . . well, because he was leading me to you."

With tears in his eyes, he draws her in for a warm embrace and whispers in her ear, "Please, tell him thank you for me."

"*Uh, yeah, you're welcome.* I need someone to take this hot mess off my hands for me," I joke as Frank pushes me.

"Don't say that. You'd be lost without her and it's so sweet. I knew he would fall hard for her."

"I know. I'm teasing. But did you see? She even admitted to giving me the silent treatment over here when I don't give her what she wants. The problem is, I am giving her what she wants, just not quick enough. I have so much more work to do."

"I feel like I've known ye forever. Like we're long lost best friends that lost touch and we're picking up right where we left off but with significant benefits, of course," Finn professes.

"I know. There's such a familiarity about you. You feel like . . . well, you feel like home to me," Hank says and he gives her a long passionate kiss.

"You have such a tender heart," Finn pauses. "This might seem crazy but my parents's thirty-fifth wedding anniversary is next weekend. I would love it if ye joined me."

"In Scotland?"

"Aye, in Scotland."

"Are you sure? Won't your parents be in shock?"

"They'll be thrilled," he assures her.

She takes a deep breath and says, "I've never said these words out loud before, maybe because I'm just acknowledging it myself, but I've been terrified to love someone as much as I loved Dan."

"I might be the only person who knows exactly how ye feel," Finn says.

"Aww, see, now don't you feel bad after that declaration of love?" Frank asks, looking over as I wipe away a tear.

"*What?* I have something in my eye," I respond.

"Uh, huh," Frank says, rubbing my back.

#

Hank and Finn are on their way to Scotland. Frank sends them off with a rainbow outside their plane window. They are half way over the Atlantic before Hank's internal panic attack starts. Fortunately, Finn is well into a nap.

Danny, how is this happening? How did I get myself into this dilemma? Here I am, on a plane, after only knowing him a few weeks, on the way to meet his parents. I haven't thought about the magnitude of what this means. I'm immersing myself deeper and deeper into this "hooking up with Mac" lie. If he ever finds out, now his parents will be involved. What would they think of me? What will they think of me is the better question. I know very little about Christine. Will I measure up? What was she like? I don't even know the shoes I'm trying to fill. I mean, was she kind? Generous? Thoughtful? Oh my God, was she hot? Why have I not realized how big of a deal this is? I've been swept up in this fun, steamy, romance without looking at the bigger picture. He's taking me to Scotland to meet his parents. The first woman they will be meeting since . . . they helped their son bury his wife.

"Can someone please release an oxygen mask from the overhead bin or maybe the flight attendant can serve up some Xanax. *Hank. You must chill.*" I turn to Frank. "I mean, do you think there is a way I can cause momentary turbulence? Just enough so her head hits the back of the drink tray and knocks some sense into her?"

"Stop it, you," Frank laughs. "She knows this is a huge deal. His parents will love her. She has nothing to worry about."

They travel overnight, so they arrive midafternoon the next day, Scottish time. Finn is surprising his parents, so they need to keep a low profile over the next twenty-four hours. They go straight to the hotel to check in.

"Get settled in, Liv. I'm going to sneak over to the club to meet with the manager and make sure everything is taken care of for tomorrow. Do ye need anything before I go?" he asks.

"No, I'm good. I'm looking forward to a shower and some sleep."

"Yes, ye should try to get some sleep so yer not too jet lagged tomorrow. I'll wake ye up when I get back and we can head to dinner. How does that sound?"

"Sounds perfect," she says.

That is until she starts to unpack her suitcase and notices a very strong floral odor. It smells like someone poured a ten-gallon bucket of air freshener all over her stuff. She identifies the problem.

"Really Hank, you packed *Poo-Pourri?*" I say. "This man has seen your every nook and cranny and you're worried about pooping around him? I hate to burst your bubble but wait until he wakes up tonight, at three a.m. with explosive diarrhea. He'll be four feet away from your bed, in that tiny phone booth of a bathroom, with a paper-thin door where it will sound like the toilet bowl is going to crack from the air pressure."

"Gross," Frank says.

"Is this really what women worry about? I mean, I had two sisters and had no idea this is the kind of stuff that was running around in their head."

"Well, yes. It's important we maintain a certain image," she says.

"She's wiped out twice already. Pretty sure that dainty flower-girl image has long passed."

"Give her a break," Frank scolds.

#

They arrive early afternoon on the day of the party to check the set-up progress. The party is at the golf course where Finn and Mac worked in high school. They arrive at the club house, and he leads her into the main dining room. He heads back to the kitchen to throw his weight around and she starts making her way through the memories. His parents's friends collected old photos. There are framed portraits and poster boards surrounding the head table. She's excited to know everything about Finn. His family, his childhood, Christine. She approaches the table to find pictures of baby Finn. He's chubby but super smiley with huge dimples, tiny freckles and sparkly eyes, just adorable. You can tell even from this young age he is going to go on in life to do great things. She makes her way through the awkward primary school class sections to his secondary school graduation picture. So handsome. She's gaining the courage to move over to the Christine section when her butterflies kick in.

"This is going to be *epic*," I say.

"They are going to *freak* when they find out we know each other. I can barely contain myself," Frank says.

"Here we go," I say just as Hank's eyes shift to focus on the next picture. It's a photograph of Christine, Finn, and Dan, from Ireland. *Oh. My. God. Christine is Frank. Impossible.*

She has to grab the table to prevent herself from collapsing. Just as Finn is making his way back over to her, he notices the tears.

"Liv, love, what's the matter?" he presses.

She can barely get the words out.

"Finn, oh my God. Christine . . . She"s Frank . . . Mary Christine Frances."

"Aye, but how on earth did you figure that out?"

She points to the photograph. "Because this is Dan, MY Dan. Frank's Dan; he's the one who died."

"Bloody hell, Liv . . . Jesssuuus . . ." Aghast, he paces back and forth, his hands on his brow.

"I couldn't find Frank to tell her about the accident," she whimpers.

"He never made it to our wedding. I cannot believe this. I should have known. That day when ye walked in with your claddagh necklace. Frank had the exact same one. It was a gift from Dan when we traveled in Ireland. He bought an identical one for his best friend, Hank, at home. Of course, Olivia Henry . . . Hank."

And she begins to sob.

"And you are never going to believe this; I had my sister, Jane, ship out the photo album Frank made him from your trip because I wanted to show you what he looked like. It's in my suitcase back at the hotel. I was waiting for the right time to show you. Now I'm realizing there were pictures with Frank's boyfriend . . . that was you."

He reaches out to embrace her and whispers, "He's exactly how ye described him, Liv. Darling, I am soo, soo sorry."

"These are actually happy tears, Finn. I can't believe you met him. This is beyond belief. It's been them all along. They've been orchestrating our meeting from the other side."

"Uncanny and remarkable."

They managed to pull themselves together in plenty of time for the party to begin. His parents are thrilled to see his face and even more pleased to see his smile, knowing he has again found happiness. They welcome Hank with open arms. They tell them about the amazing connection they just uncovered, and they are rendered speechless. It is truly a time for celebration and they are more than happy to oblige.

#

They race back to the hotel and Hank pulls out the photo album. They sit and cry as they thumb through each of the photos, knowing how much love we had for each of them and the loss we both endured. They're both overwhelmed as they lay there in silence, holding each other, realizing how incredibly lucky and grateful they are.

"Finn, I have to tell you something," Hank whispers.

"What is it, love?" Finn says as he strokes and caress her soft skin.

"This might sound really weird and I don't know if you even believe in this, but have you ever heard of a medium? You know, someone who's able to connect with people on the other side?"

"Aye, I've seen the TV shows."

"Remember the first night you made me dinner at the restaurant?"

"Aye."

"Well, on a whim, I stopped in to see a medium that day. I was coming out of the hair salon and saw a sign for readings and walked in. I've never done anything like that before so I was somewhat skeptical. Before I went in, I asked Dan to have the medium say something specific, so I would know it was really him if he showed up."

"And?"

"Dan came through loud and clear. The medium asked me if his name was Hank."

"I'm flummoxed."

"Yes, I couldn't believe it. It was crazy but so wonderful and reaffirmed what I already knew deep down. But there was something else. She also kept saying there was a woman there with him and she knows you. Of course, I had no idea who she could be referring to. I didn't know anyone else who was young who had passed away but now I know — it was Christine. She's with Dan. The medium said they were laughing and being silly. Then she said, they want you to know they will always be with you and watching out for you."

"Jesus, Liv. Ye keep taking my breath away."

"I know. I wasn't ever planning on sharing it with anyone, but that message was for you, too."

"It's bloody fantastic to know they're together and taking care of each other."

"Heartwarming," she says, consumed with emotion as they drift off to sleep.

#

ENTRY #7

> *My beloved Hank,*
>
> *Wow! WHAT A DAY! We did it!! Frank and I cried happy tears, witnessing the moment. We rented out McGee's and had bottles and bottles of champagne to celebrate the milestone. No one could believe we pulled it off. This plan has been in motion for years. If you knew what went into ensuring all of this revealed itself at the perfect time, you'd be floored. We are pretty much heroes within the Angel community. Everyone has been asking us to give them a copy of our blueprints, so they can replicate the idea. The problem is, this is a once in a lifetime plan. It can't be repeated. It's your story— meant for you and Finn. Frank and I are honored we got to be the ones to orchestrate it. You must B E L I E V E.*
>
> *Anyway, more soon.*
>
> *I love you forever and always,*
>
> *Danny*

CHAPTER ELEVEN

"Today's another big day," Frank says.

"Oh yeah, how so?" I ask.

"Finn has another surprise up his sleeve. He's surprising Hank with a trip to Paris. Now that they realize our connection, Finn is ready to move on and wants to share the life he had with me, back in Paris. To move on with Hank, he needs closure. This is his first time back since I passed."

"Wow. Hank will understand the intensity of the circumstances."

"He has the perfect day planned for her. . . "

\#

They catch a train to Paris and arrive at the apartment in time for dinner and a good night's sleep. Hank is still jet lagged from the time change. Plus, it's been an emotional trip.

"Morning, ye look glorious." Finn teases her as he holds his hands behind Hank's back.

"Whatcha got there?" she says playfully as he pulls out a wrapped gift.

"Yer future. I hope you like it," he replies, handing it to her.

"Finn McDaniels. I'm touched. This is amazing," she responds, teary as she unwraps the baby blue journal he bought for her. It's inscribed — *Let the Sparks Fly* in gold lettering.

"This is inspiration for yer new career. It's a journal for you to start writing."

"It's perfect. Thank you." She reaches out and takes a handful of his shirt, pulling him in for a kiss. "Mmmm, as much as I don't want this to end, we have a busy day ahead, so let's go."

Their first stop is Benoit. He introduces her around to all the staff to show her where he got his start. Then they head over to the café where he met Frank. Next up is the Eiffel Tower, right at sunset, where they share a perfect kiss. They cover many of the firsts he had with Frank, so he can now replace the devastating memories with happy ones, including Hank.

The next and final stop, however, will forever be just their own. It's a beautiful, clear day with a touch of chill in the air, enough to feel alive. He leads her onto the Love Lock Bridge. There are boats passing in both directions on the river and about two dozen other couples spread out across the bridge. Finn tells Hank to close her eyes and leads her to the spot. When she opens them up, he presents her with a small box.

"I realize we've only known each other for a short time, but ye are an absolute gift to me, Liv. Ye've reignited a spark in me. I feel so alive again, maybe more alive than I've ever felt. Knowing that Dan and Christine are behind all of this makes it that much more extraordinary. Love was the furthest thing from my mind when ye *fell* into my life. Sorry, couldn't resist," he says, and she chuckles. "I never thought I'd find love again and never dreamed of something this incredible. The intensity. The intimacy. Ye get me. Ye fit. I want ye to know how much I cherish ye and treasure our connection."

Tears start streaming from her eyes.

"Finn, I've been closed off from love for so long. A huge piece of my heart died when I lost Dan. You are the only one who has been able to fill that gaping hole. Since I met you, I've let go of all my inhibitions. You have melted all my impenetrable walls. You've healed all my wounds. You've restored faith, hope and love in me. I feel like my life is just beginning. I don't know where it's going to take us, but I know I want to start the journey with you by my side. In many ways, it scares me to death, but I'm ready to jump into this with both feet," she says as the perfect Paris scenery fades in the background. He hands her the heart-shaped, sterling silver necklace from the palm of his hand.

"This is a love locket I bought for ye that I want ye to wear forever and always. I will wear the other half, which is the key that opens it. I am eternally grateful that ye've given me the honor and privilege of unlocking yer heart to love again."

Her eyes begin streaming with tears.

"Oh, Finn."

"That's not all. We're standing on the Lovers Lock Bridge. Couples have been coming here for well over a century to profess their love to one another. The tradition is to place locks on the bridge, symbolizing a promise to always be together." He reaches into his pocket and pulls out four locks.

"Why are there four?"

"One for you, me, Dan, and Christine."

"Finn, oh my God . . . this is so touching." Hank interlocks all the locks together. They claim a spot on the bridge, and he hands her the keys.

"Now ye have to make a wish as ye throw the keys into the river."

"Okay, but I'm saying it to myself or else the wish won't come true." She closes her eyes.

Danny, you overwhelm me. I'm so glad you're up there with Christine. It all makes sense now. The struggle, the pain, the wait has been worth every second of every minute of every day. I wouldn't change one thing. I know you will continue to watch over us, and know that I will love you, forever. I am grateful for Finn; you found the other half of me.

She throws the keys over her left shoulder before she and Finn share a tender kiss. They return to the apartment exhausted but giddy. Finn begins to prepare dinner and she props herself front and center at the kitchen island to watch him work his magic.

Danny, today was the perfect day. I'm grateful he is opening up to me and allowing me in. I could never have predicted this in my wildest dreams. Less than a month ago, I was going through the motions, putting one foot in front of the other. Living day to day, hour by hour with no clear direction on where I was heading.

She's suddenly overcome with emotion as she's thinking about all the events that had to align to get them to this place.

"Wait for it, Danny, this is for you . . . " Frank says.

Hank opens her journal to start the first chapter of her story, the title . . . *The Man Guide.*

"*What?*" I squawk in disbelief.

"Yes, all of this is inspiring her to write. You did it. She's crossing the bridge to her bigger purpose."

"I'm speechless but *The Man Guide?*" I pause. "I mean, I know that is the name on the journal *Chuy* gave me to use as my journal diary to Hank."

"Yes, you're him. She's going to tell the story about a woman whose life keeps hitting dead ends until she takes the advice of her guardian angel . . . her man guide," Frank says.

"Aww . . . that's *so* amazing." I'm all choked up.

"Yep, *Chuy* still has some beautiful surprises in store for us up here."

#

Frank finishes ordering a round of beers, and I place my order for the best tuna melt and waffle fries there is when Jake joins us at McGee's. We're moving onto the next phase of the project. Unfortunately, having Hank and Finn meet is the *easy* part of this process. We still have a long way to go. We're fueling up as we regroup. Time for reinforcements.

"It's hard watching Hank and Finn peel themselves away from each other, so she can go back to close her life up in Chicago," Frank says as we monitor their parting at the airport.

"I know and this is *not* going to be easy," I say.

"Hank thinks she's over the hump and we still have a long way to go."

"Indeed. But her friends: Liza, Alexa along with Red, Jane and Garrett will get her through."

"*Wait*, did you say Liza?" Jake interrupts. "As in, Liza Sanders?"

"Yes, why? Do you know her?" I ask.

"Yes, she's one of my closest buddies from the UK. She's hilarious," he says. "How does she fit in here?"

"She's sitting next to Hank on her flight back to Chicago. Hank is going back to put her condo up for sale, so she can move out to Palm Springs to be with Finn full-time. They figure out that Liza's cousin,

Alexa, is a good friend of Hank's from college. You got all that?" I pause.

"Liza, cousins with Alexa . . . Hank's college buddy. Got it," Jake says.

"She's going to reconnect with these girls. They're going to be a special part of her life moving forward. Starting this weekend. They're going to bond at the Journey concert. Concerts are going to be their *thing*. There will be a special concert soon that will be critical for her to attend, and they are the only ones who will convince her to go."

"Wait, *Journey* . . . that's the name of my journal," he says.

"We just figured out the meaning of ours," I say, filling Jake in on *The Gift* and *The Man Guide*.

"Buckle up. Things are about to get bumpy and Liza is a key part of helping Hank get through it," I say.

#

"Liv, don't freak out, but we're at the hospital with Owen," Jane says.

"What? Oh my God. Why?"

"He's been throwing up since we got home from Dad's party yesterday. We thought it might be something he ate, but it hasn't stopped so we came to the ER to make sure he isn't dehydrated."

"Is Livey okay? Do you think it's a bug?"

"No, Livey isn't sick. Mom and Dad came over, so she could sleep."

"Is it something serious with Owen?"

"The doctors are now recommending he be transferred to Children's Hospital downtown. They don't know what's wrong, but they want him down there, so he can be evaluated and monitored. They're taking him by ambulance."

"Oh dear God. How are you holding up? Because I am completely freaking out."

"I know. Just please meet us over there," she whispers, trying to hold back her emotion.

Jane is very calm, while Hank is a mess hearing the news that her beautiful, sweet, and innocent two-year-old nephew is en route to a children's hospital.

"Okay. I'm on my way." She hangs up to throw some clothes on and order an Uber.

Danny, we have a deal, remember? When the twins were born, I told you I would never get married if you watched over them and kept them safe and healthy. Now I've met Finn, so what? The deal is off? I don't plan to trade one for the other, so don't force me to choose. I need to hear "Small Town" stat. I need to know Owen will be okay.

"Hank, I'm *right* here. Here you go."

She finds "Small Town" on the XM Radio in the Uber. "Breathe. He's going to be fine . . . lean on me," I say.

She arrives at the hospital and meets with Jane then calls Finn while they await Owen's room assignment.

"Finn . . ." she whimpers.

"*Bloody hell* . . . what is it?" He senses the quivering in her voice.

"It's Owen. He's in the hospital," she says then bursts into tears.

"How's everyone holding up?"

"Everyone is okay. I'm the biggest wreck. *Shocker.* I just can't . . ."

He interrupts, "I know Liv, I know. I'm already sending a special request to Christine to watch over him, too."

"Thank you. I have Dan all over it. I heard "Small Town" on my way over in the Uber, which provided some relief. I'm going out to Jane's house to relieve my parents and spend the night with little Livey. By the way, on a happy note, I finally told everyone all about you. They can't wait to meet you," she says, trying to maintain some positivity.

"I wish I could drive over to be with you. Text me when you get to your sister's. Keep me posted."

"I will. By the way, I hate to even say this out loud, but, you know, they say things come in threes, like bad news or worse . . . death. First, it's Owen. I don't even want to think about what the next thing could be."

"Don't even go there. Get some rest. I miss you," Finn says.

"I miss you, too," she responds, reluctant to let him go.

"Finn's going to get on the next flight to Chicago to be with her," Frank says. "He's shaken. He hasn't gotten a call like this since . . . well, since *my* news. He's going to want to be with her, to comfort her. He'll use it as an excuse to go on to Paris to start cleaning out the apartment, plus he needs to renew his passport and visa."

"Hank is on her way to the cemetery to beg and plead with me. She thinks a personal visit is going to get me to respond quicker. She needs to learn I'm with her everywhere," I say. "The silver lining here is that she is going to throw herself into writing to relieve her anxiety. It's her escape. I'm so glad she's tapping into her passion. It will make all of the difference in her life."

Finn pulls off the surprise without a hitch. It's not the ideal 'meeting the family' moment, but they are all touched that he would come all this way to be with Hank. Now he's had the chance to meet everyone and see her life here in Chicago, so he can envision her surroundings when he's talking to her long distance. They found out Owen had a bad case of strep that attacked his kidneys, so he's on a strong dose of antibiotics and should be back to normal in about a week. Finn's now on his leg to Paris.

#

Hank gets a cryptic text from Jane and catapults out of bed and charges to the living room, scrambling for the remote. Splashed over every TV channel are images of a terrorist attack at the Charles de Gaulle Airport. The airport in Paris where Finn is landing.

Oh my God, this is number two. No, no, no, no this can't be happening.

She collapses, sobbing and gripping her phone, willing it to ring.

Ring! Ring! GOD DAMMIT RING! Dear God. Please. Don't you DARE do this to me, Danny. I will never survive this. Never. I can't do it again. She frantically texts Finn. She lays on the ground waiting for news, on the verge of vomiting, praying for a response. Changing channels to see if there's any different coverage. Every news outlet is running an endless loop of footage of the bomb going off, but you can't make out anyone in the crowd or see any damage, just an explosion followed by a plume of smoke. All flights both domestic and international are grounded until they determine if the threat is contained. Hank tries to talk herself off the ledge.

Take a deep breath. Maybe his battery died or he's still in the air, so his phone is turned off. I mean, what are the odds of being in a terrorist attack? One in fifty million? Of course, Finn is safe. He must be. There's no other option. What are the chances he was in the area at the exact moment the bombs detonated? I'm sure he hasn't called because service is down in the area with all the chaos.

She directs her attention back to the TV. There were two bombers. The explosives went off in the baggage claim area forty-five seconds apart. She's waiting for the death and injury count to scroll across the screen. CNN reports at least sixty-three people are dead, and at least one hundred more are injured, some severely.

Oh my God. No one even knows to look for him. I'm not even sure he told anyone other than Tex and me that he was heading to Paris. I need to get in touch with Mac. His parents. I don't have anyone's number. I feel so powerless.

She calls Garrett and has him go to the restaurant to get in touch with Tex, who has numbers for everyone as Jane and Red arrive at the condo, doing everything in their power to comfort Hank, but it's hopeless. Her phone rings.

"It's an unknown number," Red says as she quickly passes Hank the phone.

"Finn, Finn is that you?" she asks desperately.

"Olivia. It's Mac. Finn's friend. Your cousin Garrett asked me to call you," he says.

"Mac, yes, hi," she responds, pretending to have no idea who he is. "Have you heard anything?"

"Naw, but his mum and da are driving down to Paris now," he says. "His mum called the airline, but since the explosion happened in the airport they cannot be certain who, if anyone, was involved from his flight. They only have the manifest stating he was on the flight. Other than that, I don't have any news. It will be tomorrow before they arrive, so we won't know anything until then."

"Please, keep me posted," she begs.

"Aye, ye as well," he says.

"Red, can you get online and book me on the next available flight to Paris, which is probably days away at this point, but I can't sit here. I'm going over there."

"Get your passport. I'll need to add it for TSA," Red says, grabbing the computer and wasting no time.

"Liv . . . " she stumbles.

"What? I don't care how much it costs. Just book it," she insists.

"No. It's your passport. It expires in a couple months. They won't let you fly," she says, trying to break the news delicately.

"Why is this happening to me? Now what? I have to sit in this condo, for God knows how long, desperately awaiting any news. And God forbid it's bad news. Then what? I can't even go over there to be with him. This is unbelievable." She throws her hands up in frustration. "Is this some sort of joke, Dan? Why are you doing this to me? You introduce me to the love of my life then completely rip the rug out from under me. What is wrong with you? This can't be part of God's plan. Part of my plan. He can't be this cruel. I can't do it. I won't do it. God should know. He gave me this heart. He knows I can't do this again. Never again. You and Christine have to be with him. *Please*. Protect him. Please, please make him be okay," Hank pleads.

"Oh, this is a rough one, Danny," Frank says.

"I know, my best hope is to channel through Red right now. She is the calm, reasonable one. I need her to manage this one on the ground. She knows me. She must know I would never let anything terrible happen. I'd negotiate something with *Chuy*. Hank can't handle this. She won't survive it. *Come on, Red.* Help me out here . . ."

"I'm going to use my super sign to visit Finn. He's unconscious so I want to reassure him I'm there. I need to tell him it's all going to be okay," Frank says.

"You sure you want to cash it in now? You only get the one."

"I know, but this is the closest he's going to get to here. It's the best time for me to reach him."

"Okay, well, good luck. I have to save mine. This event still isn't the worst of it."

"Liv . . . come on. You can't do this to yourself. You've been glued to this TV all day. You need to settle yourself down and get some sleep. There's nothing we can do but wait. You haven't eaten anything. Dan and Christine are looking out for him. We'll have answers soon. Jane and I will stay up and wait for any calls. We promise to wake you up the *second* we hear anything," Red says, rubbing Hank's back and nudging Hank toward her room.

"Dan knows how impatient I am. How much I worry. The unknown is the worst place for me to be."

"You know the other thing about the unknown? It could also be good news. Let's hope and pray for the best. You'll be thinking more clearly after you get some sleep," Red says as she tucks Hank into bed.

"Go, Red," Frank cheers.

"I know. She's the only thing that saved Hank when I crossed over. She has this calming presence. She knows exactly what to say to talk her off the ledge. Hank always goes to the worst-case scenario. I need to find a way to break her of that."

"Time and patience are the only two variables that will help her," Frank offers.

"She completely sucks at both. Ugh." I say, throwing my hands up.

#

The phone rings early the next morning, and Hank leaps out of bed to answer. It's Mac.

"They found him. He's in a hospital about ten miles from the airport. Based on his injuries, they think he was within a few hundred feet of the blast. He must have been separated from all his things because he didn't have any ID on him. He was unconscious when he arrived, so they didn't have any way to identify him," he explains.

"Oh my God. How bad is it?" Hank says, dropping to her knees.

"He's going to be fine. They think he was knocked out with the impact, but then his body went into shock. They put him in a medically induced coma to keep the swelling down. They've done several brain scans, and everything looks fine. So outside of several nasty gashes, three broken ribs, a separated shoulder, a bruised tailbone, and two black eyes, he is expected to make a full recovery. His parents plan to stay with him to nurse him through recovery."

"Oh thank God, Mac. I just couldn't imagine . . ."

"Aye. I'll ring you again in the mornin'," he says as they hang up. Red knows instantly it's good news as Hank collapses into her arms.

"He was only in Chicago for me. He came to support me. He would never have been on that plane if it weren't for me. I won't be able to live with myself . . ." She breaks down.

"Liv. Stop. You can't go there. You can't continue to live in fear. I know Dan; he's up there watching out for Finn for you. You must believe that. Trust him. No one loved you more than Dan. He was so protective of you. He's your own personal guardian angel. He talks to you more than I do, for God's sake. He would never take Finn away from you. You so deserve this happiness. It won't end this way. You have to keep the faith. This is the beginning for you," Red asserts as she makes her way to the kitchen to make some breakfast.

"I want to believe that with every ounce of my being, but I'm so scared. I've been so closed off from love for years for this exact reason. I let my guard down and let someone in. The perfect complement to me. He's my best friend. He's repaired the huge gaping hole in my heart since losing Dan," Hanks says.

"He's going to be *fine*. Believe."

Danny. Will you forgive me? I am so sorry I doubted you. I just . . . well, you know. I just couldn't. I couldn't lose you twice. You know I love you, forever.

#

ENTRY #8

My beloved Hank,

Just when I thought it couldn't get worse, the unthinkable happens. This life thing is a crazy rollercoaster and you are not having any fun at it. I have to say; today I'm most thankful for Red. I love you more than anything, but she keeps her wits about her — always. I don't think I ever knew to appreciate this about her when I was there. What a beautiful quality. She has the power to snap you back to reality. Faith, my dear, you need to find it.

Anyway, more soon.

I love you forever and always,

Danny

CHAPTER TWELVE

I schedule my next meeting with *Chuy*.

"Daniel, My son. Please come in," HE greets me as I approach his office. "What can I do for you?"

"Can I be frank with you?" I ask.

"Of course. I would expect nothing less."

"I want to punch her in the throat. There, I said it."

"*Dory?*" HE asks.

"Uhhh, yeah. She is *not getting it*. It's so frustrating. It's three steps forward then twenty-two steps back. I'm constantly reassuring her. I send her at least one to two signs a day and not *little* signs. These are EPIC. She hangs on for a millisecond and then it's right back to square one," I explain.

"Welcome to MY world, son."

"Oh right, I forget Who I'm talking to. I only have her, and You have all of mankind. Honestly, props to You because this is exhausting."

"The primary virtue you're trying to teach her is *patience*."

"Couldn't You have given me empathy or compassion? Those are easypeasy. Patience is nearly impossible."

"You need to teach her. Lead by example. Remember, you're asking her to believe in something she has no proof of. Of course, she wants nothing more than to feel your presence or believe you are with her, but you need to give her time. I promise you, she'll come around. Take it one day and one sign at a time.

Just be there for her. She and Finn will be tested. They're both terrified. They've both experienced tremendous loss. They've lost their confidence. They have doubts. As good as it feels, they are questioning whether they should trust how magical this feels. If I give them everything now, they'll be content with love alone. Both need time to focus on their own passions and not lose sight of themselves. They are both destined for big things. I need them to work hard and dig deep and work it out within themselves. You know her, she found Finn. What is her next move?"

"To pack up her life and move to be with him."

"Right. And once she gets there, what will she do?"

"She'll pour herself into making him the happiest man alive. She'll support his business and do whatever she can to make him a success."

"Exactly. But what about her destiny? Do you think she'll pursue writing?"

"Well, no . . . "

"Why do you think that is?"

"Because she uses writing as an escape when she's scared."

"Okay, has she written lately?"

"Yes, she wrote several chapters when Owen was in the hospital."

"And what do you think she is going to do while Finn is recovering?"

"She's going to write to pass the time, to make it go faster. It's the only thing that relieves her anxiety."

"Do you know why?"

"Because she connects with me when she's writing and I bring her comfort."

"Exactly. And do you know what's going to happen once she finishes that manuscript?"

"No."

"It's going to turn into a movie."

"Wow. Really?"

"Yes. You see, many people don't understand My love and the ways in which I work. I know the unique approach to get through to each of you. Only one formula per person. For her, it's through deprivation. She's selfless. If I give her what she wants, she'll focus on others and not herself. Yes, she wants Finn, but she'll lose herself in his dream. She needs to see her dreams through first."

"Huh. I think You're on to something there."

It didn't dawn on me until now, but *HE*'s right. Finn professed his love for her, she got a window into his life, hers is in shambles, and so she got on the next plane to go pack up her life and move away without hesitation. She'd give him every ounce of herself to help him succeed. But what about her? She's willing to abandon her passion. She'll write it off in her head as a hobby and get to it when she gets to it because she doesn't know it's her destiny.

"This will all happen . . . but in My time. Not hers. She has work to do first. You see, there isn't any other one person that can complete you. You need to complete yourself first. This is the beginning of their amazing love story. I created their souls to be together. Now get back to her and teach her patience."

"How will I know when I succeeded?" I say as I turn to leave.

"She will tell you."

"Thanks, *Chuy*. I don't know if anyone has told You today but *You rock!*" I say over my shoulder.

"Thank you, Daniel." *HE* pauses. "Oh and one more thing . . . "

"Yes." I stop dead in my tracks, waiting to be scolded.

"I saw you push her. Nice work." *HE* laughs.

#

It's been six long weeks of recovery for Finn but he's on the mend. Once his body can handle the long flight to the States, he is on his way to Hank. She will finish nursing him back to health. She picks him up at the airport. She tears up the moment their eyes meet.

"Can I hug you?" she says.

"Aye, I want nothing more than to be in those arms," he says, leaning over for an embrace. "Just be gentle," he whispers.

"I plan to wait on you hand and foot. Let's get you home and comfortable." She reaches for his arm to guide him out of the airport. She gets him settled in at the condo before she shares the good news.

"I have a few updates to share with you. I waited to tell you in person. I wanted to surprise you."

"Aye . . . ?"

"First . . . I've spent the last six weeks writing my manuscript, *The Man Guide*. Without a job and being away from you, I had to find a way to channel my anxiety and nervous energy. Writing is my escape. It helps pass the time and is cathartic."

"That's bloody fantastic. Are ye done?" He grabs her hand, pulling her down for a kiss. "I'm so proud of you, Liv."

"Is it ever really done? This might sound crazy, but I think I was born to do this."

"Naw, not crazy at all. That's how I became a chef. I used to help my mum cook when I was growing up, but it was never work; it was fun. That's the difference between a job and the dream — yer passionate about it. Passion is what drives and motivates ye."

"I never thought about it that way. I guess I followed the path set in front of me without question. I went through the motions. Once my career fell apart, I started looking at things differently. I'm amazed at what all the turmoil has uncovered," she gushes. "Very unexpected . . . like meeting you."

"*HE* was right," I say to Frank.

"Who?" she says.

"*Chuy. HE* told me Hank would dive into her writing while Finn was recovering. Amazing. And look at her light up. She's glowing. She's so excited to tell him about it. I had no idea she had this story inside of her."

"If you think about it, she has the best of both worlds," Frank says.

"How so?"

"She has both of her favorite men with her. She's channeling you, so she can get to him."

"Huh, I never thought about it that way."

"Writing allows her to keep you alive and with her forever."

#

"The best news is, I sold the condo. I close in two weeks." She wraps her arms around Finn.

"Brilliant. Best news I could ever ask for."

"I know. Now we can road trip out West but first, a toast." She raises her glass. "To never scaring the shit out of me again."

"Aye, and you either," Fin agrees.

129

"I mean, if you wanted to break up with me, there were much easier ways," she jokes.

"I don't ever want to leave you again, Liv." A tear rolls down his cheek. "We've both been through so much. Let's pray this is a fresh start. A beautiful new beginning of only good things."

"We have faith that Dan and Christine are with us, sending us signs and watching over us. I have no doubt they are the only reason I am sitting here today. I believe they protected me during the attack. I've now seen the footage and the damage. It's a miracle I walked away," he says, his gratitude evident. "Remember how they put me into a medically induced coma when I first arrived at the hospital?"

"Yes," she says.

"I'm having flashbacks. The doctors warned me it could happen since my body went into shock. My brain suppressed the event. They said certain things might trigger my memory and images might re-surface, helping me to put the pieces of the puzzle back together."

"What? Why didn't you say something sooner?" she says with concern in her voice.

"It's only happened a couple times, but it's what I'm remembering that's startling," he continues. "The flashback is an image of Christine appearing over me just after the bomb went off. She said, *Believe in me. Everything will be okay.* She hugged me and left."

"Finn, that's incredible," she says, getting emotional. "What did she look like?"

"I can't make out her face or body. It was a silhouette and her voice. Do you think I'm imagining it? Maybe it was a dream?"

"I believe with everything in my soul that was her. No question. Dan was probably standing right behind her. I have chills running through my entire body."

Frank and I high five.

"We're getting closer," she says.

"Only one more major hurdle."

#

Today is their last day on the road trip. The closer they get to LA, the more Hank's paranoia sets in. Tonight, they are staying with Mac and Jules. Meeting is inevitable.

What if Mac does recognize me? Is our secret going to be outed the minute he opens the door? I'm praying he doesn't remember anything. He's a big celebrity now. I'm sure he had his fair share of one-night stands. I'm just another notch on the bedpost. I mean, I'm good in bed, but I don't think our night was anything magical.

"Liv, are ye okay? Yer quiet this morning." Finn reaches over and grabs her hand. "Are ye daydreaming? Mentally finishing that manuscript?" He smiles.

"I think all the driving is catching up to me, plus you didn't give me much time to sleep last night," Hank says, trying to pull off a nonchalant vibe. Finn is sensing her mood.

They pull up to Mac's gate. Finn calls up to the house for them to be buzzed in. Jules comes running from the house, waving her hands in excitement. Finn rolls down the window to greet her as she leans in to give him a kiss on the cheek.

"Olivia, I can't contain myself any longer. We've heard so much about you," she says as she runs over to

Hank's side of the car. God, I hope she still feels that way in two minutes when she meets Mac, who is right on her heels.

"I'm a hugger; I hope that's okay?" she asks mid-hug.

"Of course, me, too. So great to meet you," Hank responds as she sees Mac approaching out of the corner of her eye.

"Aye lassie, we've heard so much about ye. Pleasure to meet ye," Mac says as she studies him to see if he has any mental triggers going off.

Annnnnnnnnnd we're clear. He is an actor, so maybe he's good at hiding his facial expressions. Either way, I'm going to go with . . . he doesn't remember me.

Mac and Jules lead them into the house. Finn insists on making dinner. He's itching to get back into the kitchen. This is the perfect opportunity to test his stamina. See how long he can be on his feet and determine the range of motion. Wine is flowing. Hank already feels like she's known these these two her whole life as they swap story after story. They remind her of her friendship with Red. She's trying to suppress the Mac guilt, but the twinge lingers.

"Liv, you're pretty funny," Mac says.

"That's quite the compliment coming from you when you've made a career of it," she says, afraid of what's coming next.

Finn's face lights up. "I cannot believe I haven't told ye, but Liv also took classes at Second City, but in Chicago. In fact, it was probably right about the same time ye were in New York, Mac. Isn't that crazy?" Finn glances over at Mac and sees the lightbulb go off. "In fact, she's taken such a liking to it she began writing her own manuscript. Go on, tell him, Liv," Finn encourages.

SHIT. SHIT. SHIT. Hank nervously responds, "Finn, it's not that big of a deal, really. I don't want Mac to think we came here to pitch my idea . . . it's nothing . . ."

"Ye'll have to come down to the studio and shadow the writing team for a day. It would be great exposure," Mac says.

"That's very kind of you but not necessary." Hank grabs her plate and heads toward the kitchen. "Anyone need another drink?"

"I'll come and grab a couple more bottles of wine," Mac offers as he follows her into the kitchen.

FUUUUUUUUUUUUUUUUUUUUUUUCK.

As soon they clear the wall separating the kitchen from the dining room, she hears, "Wait, yer *that* Olivia?" Mac asks in shock. "Have ye told him?"

"Hell no. Are you kidding? Do you think we'd be having dinner here right now?" she whispers, praying Finn and Jules don't walk in. "I was banking on you not remembering me."

"I remember, but that was ages ago," Mac says.

"Listen, we can't talk about this here. Not a word until we come up with a plan," she says. "Deal?"

"Deal," he says as they make their way back to join in.

The weekend continues without issue. Jules shares with them that her brother has been diagnosed with ALS. She and Hank decide to throw him a fundraiser at Christine's to raise money. While she is distracted, Finn plans a big party for Hank's birthday. He's flying Red out, but the big surprise is VIP tickets to the John Mellencamp concert, including a meet and greet.

#

Hank arrives at the studio and Mac greets her.

"Hi, Mac. I'm touched; thank you for having me."

"Aye, ye are my best bloke's lass and are helping Jules with the ALS fundraiser. It's the least I can do," he adds.

"About that . . ." I say as he interrupts.

"We'll talk about it afterward," he says as the rest of the team makes their way into the room. Mac introduces me to the group, and they are off to the races. They start by brainstorming and white boarding ideas while passing endless rounds of chips and sour gummy bears. She has no idea what goes into the writing, planning, and shooting of one episode. She has a newfound, deep respect and appreciation for the entertainment industry. They break for lunch, and Mac and she go back to his trailer to talk.

"Liv, I'm just as shocked at the irony. I mean, what are the chances, but I don't think we need to make this a big deal. It was one drunk night, ages ago, and was meaningless. No offense," Mac says.

"I completely agree, but I feel like it's this epic secret between Finn and me. I don't want to keep anything from him. I can't. You're his best friend," she states. "It's not right to keep this from him, and I know he senses something is off."

"Aye, it's yer decision. Don't fret. That bastard can't live without ye. I know that fer sure," Mac finishes, and they go back to meet the group for their afternoon session.

He makes an announcement.

"Team, the reason I invited Olivia to come in today is for her see this process in action. Turns out she's writing a manuscript. I thought I'd give her the opportunity to pitch her idea to the group to give her some feedback. What do ye say, Liv?" he says as the group looks at her in anticipation.

Hank is caught off guard and starts to freak out.

"This is it, Hank, your BIG break . . . don't blow it. You've got this!" I say.

These people are professionals. I can't just rattle off my idea to a room full of Hollywood experts. I have no experience other than a couple paid Second City classes that I abandoned a few years ago. I mean, am I even any good at this? What if they laugh me out of the building?

Sensing her panic, Mac intervenes.

"Liv, believe it or not, we've all been where you are. We all started somewhere. We each took a giant leap off that platform, too. This is a safe audience. This is a no judgment zone. You have nothing to lose. Now, come on, pitch us."

"Okay . . . well . . . wow, I was not expecting this, but I guess . . . here goes," she begins. "I wrote a manuscript loosely based on my life about a girl who loses her best friend at a young age in a car accident. She turns to him seeking advice and guidance, wanting him to lead her to her destiny through signs and symbols from the other side. It's called . . . *The Man Guide*. She is solely focused on dating and trying to find her perfect match. Think of a storyline concept, like the movie *Bruce Almighty* with Jim Carey where he is granted with God's powers, or *The Legend of Bagger Vance* where Will Smith plays Matt Damon's golf caddy who appears from nowhere as a guide. A man she doesn't recognize shows up, out of nowhere, claiming to be her guardian angel. He tries to convince her he is here to help. The only rule is she must make her own decisions and follow her heart. She rejects the idea and refuses to believe him, but he keeps reappearing. Convinced she can control her own journey; she ignores his advice yet continues to run into dead ends. She keeps going out with the wrong men, taking the wrong jobs, and making decisions based on the life she thinks she wants. Each time she hits a brick wall, he comes back to tell her she's on the wrong path. These are tests to get her to dig deep, to listen, and to let go. His message begins to resonate, and she slowly begins making different choices. She gains so much confidence and happiness through these new decisions because they lead her down a path to fulfilling her own personal goals. In the end, she realizes that she's on a journey to find herself, and once she does, everything else falls into place." She pauses, cringing, as she awaits their feedback, having no idea what to expect. Without a hesitation or spoken word between them, they collectively stand and begin clapping.

Overwhelmed, she responds, "Really? You like it?" She wells up in tears in amazement.

"It's brilliant," Mac declares as the team nods in agreement.

Danny, this is amazing. Is this really happening?

"Indeed it is," I say, wishing I could reach out and hug her.

#

She's anxious to race home to tell Finn everything that happened today. It will be a bittersweet evening because she plans to tell him about Mac as well. Her conscience won't let her keep this from him any longer.

He's at the house when she arrives and greets her with a hug and kiss.

"I missed ye. So anxious to hear how today went." He hands her a glass of wine, gesturing for her to sit down so he can give her his full attention.

"Oh my gosh, where do I start? It exceeded all my expectations. What these writers do is nothing short of amazing. It's incredible to see how their minds work, and then to be lucky enough to sit in the room with them and witness it firsthand is a dream come true. We broke for lunch, and when we reconvened, out of nowhere and without giving me a heads up, Mac announces to the group that I wrote a manuscript. He puts me on the spot and tells me to pitch my idea to the team. I almost fainted. I was so nervous, but everyone was so gracious." I pause. "And they loved it. I can't believe it. They blew me away . . . they even gave me a standing ovation."

"Liv, that is bloody fantastic. I am so proud of you." He pulls her in for a lingering kiss when she interrupts.

"Wait, before we take this any further, there is something else I need to tell you."

"Okay . . ." he says. "What is it?"

"Before I tell you, you have to know that it has been my intention all along to tell you. I would never want to hurt you or ever intentionally deceive you . . . ever. A couple days passed, then weeks, and it just got away from me. I was afraid of how you would react, so I didn't know how to tell you. There was never a good time," I say.

"You're scaring me, Liv; what is it?" he asks.

She takes a deep breath. "So, you know I took classes at Second City?"

"Yes, of course."

"Well, one week we had a special guest instructor teach the class. After class, a bunch of us went out. I was still reeling from the loss of Dan, and I ended up getting pretty drunk."

"Okay," he replies.

"I ended up having my first and only one-night stand. I don't even remember *any* details. I woke up in the middle of the night and realized what happened and ran out. I never saw him again."

"All right . . . " he says, confused. "I don't understand why yer telling me this now. We both had lives before we met. I didn't expect ye were an angel."

"I know, but it's relevant because of who the guest instructor was." She hesitates. "It was Mac." Cringing, she waits for his response.

He stands up and starts walking away from her then turns on his heel. "Ye slept with Mac?" he blurts out in shock.

"This is why I was so afraid to tell you. I swear I don't remember one detail. It was ages ago. We were both in a blackout, and I didn't even think he would remember me. . ."

"Liv, ye lied to me. How could ye keep this from me?" he says. "I don't know what to say. . . "

"Just say you forgive me. I swear, I wanted to tell you, but there was never a good time and with everything that's happened . . . then so much time passed I didn't even know how to bring it up." Hank begs, "Finn, *please* say something. I'm so sorry. You have to believe me . . ."

"That's why ye were so quiet on the way to LA. Then ye spent the night at his house and never thought that was information I should have? Ye pretended he was a stranger. We spent five days in the car together. Not once did it occur to ye to mention it?" He's angry.

"First of all, I don't like the way you're speaking to me. Please change your tone. It was never intentional. I was scared . . . for this exact reason. Scared that you would totally overreact and shut me out."

"Maybe we don't know each other as well as we think we do. If you could keep something like this from me, what else haven't ye told me?" he says, deflated.

"I was protecting you . . . us. It meant nothing," she cries.

"This has all been moving so fast. Maybe we should take a breather and slow things down a bit. I need some time to clear my head. I think it's best if you pack some things and . . . go stay with Garrett for a little while," he says in a solemn tone.

"Finn . . . wait . . . please . . . don't do this," she pleads, reaching for him as he grabs the handle of the sliding glass door to go outside with Frank.

"I'll wait outside to give you some space," he says, and she runs to the bathroom to throw up, then collapses on the floor, sobbing. *Danny, please help me. I can't breathe.*

"You need to take this one, Frank. She's never going to listen to me," I say.

"I got it. I'm also counting on Tex to talk some sense into Finn. He can be stubborn."

#

ENTRY #9

My beloved Hank,

*Hank, stay with me. It's okay. This is a bump.
Love isn't easy. You're being tested. This is your
first fight. You're navigating these waters. You're
both vulnerable. He's reacting because he thinks
he's lost you. He doesn't care about Mac, that's
ancient history. You can't ever keep secrets. Never.
When you were with Mac, you had no idea who
Finn was. He knows that. He's heartbroken
because he never thought it was possible for you to
keep anything from him, even if you thought it was
protecting him. Deep breaths. This storm will pass,
and you'll be even stronger.*

I love you forever and always,

Danny

CHAPTER THIRTEEN

Christine, what am I doing? Help me. I feel so lost and alone. I pushed Liv away because I'm scared. It took everything I had to move on after losing you. Please help give me strength to get past all my insecurities. I'm full of doubt. I'm afraid to love so deeply again. Can she and I last a lifetime? Am I moving too fast? I thought I was sure. What if she won't take me back now that I've been a total ass? I know you sent me signs. Maybe I'm not ready to move on yet, but I can't fathom losing her, too. Please send me a sign to let me know she truly is the one for me. She is my best friend. I'm hollow without her. How could I be so childish and let my ego take over? I don't know what to do.

Finn arrives at the restaurant. He and Tex are prepping for the day.

"You seem as ornery as a mama bear with a sore teat these days. Care to share?" Tex observes.

"Can't get anything passed ye, can I?" he retorts.

"These ears may be big, but that just means they're good for listening." He gestures for Finn to take a seat as he walks toward the grill. "I reckon I'll make you some eggs and grits."

"Naw, laddie . . . " Finn discourages him when he interrupts.

"It ain't a question. It's no trouble; now start talkin'," he replies.

"I haven't talked to Liv in a couple weeks . . . " he pauses. "She told me she had a one-night stand with my Mac. It happened several years ago before I ever knew her, before Mac met Jules. Liv took writing classes at Second City, and Mac was the guest instructor for the day. The class went out for drinks afterward, and one thing lead to another."

"And you're full of piss and vinegar about it?" he responds.

"Aye. I'm not upset about the fact they had sex. I know it was meaningless and neither of them remember it. It's the fact she kept it from me all this time. I never want there to be secrets between us."

"I reckon Liv was scared to tell ya for exactly this reason, and you went and proved her right. So, I'll make this easy for you. There's only one question to answer."

"What's that?" Finn inquires just as their restaurant manager, Mickey, appears.

"Sorry to interrupt, but I just found this on the floor in the office. What do you want me to do with it?" Mickey asks.

"What is it?" Finn asks. Tex hands him a necklace. "It's the locket necklace I surprised Liv with in Paris. I took her to the famous Love Lock Bridge when we visited after my parents's anniversary party. She wears it all the time. It must have fallen off when she was back in the office working with Jules."

This is it. This is my sign. Thank you, love, I say to Christine.

"I've gotta go, Tex. Can you cover?" Finn says.

"Git,"Tex says.

He gets in his car and goes straight to Gin & Tonic to see Garrett. He's cordial when he extends his hand. Garrett knows Finn is the man of Hank's dreams, so he wants nothing more than to see them back together.

"What's up?" Garrett asks.

"First, how is Liv?" Finn asks.

"She's a train wreck. Barely leaving the house. I've never seen her like this," he admits. "The first real glimmer of hope I've seen is Liv agreeing to meet her girlfriends for the Mellencamp concert in a couple weeks. She hasn't told them about your break. She's really isolated herself."

"Aye. If it makes ye feel any better, I'm just as destroyed. This whole thing got blown out of proportion, and it's all my fault."

"Finn, I gotta tell you . . . it meant nothing. She made herself sick over it. She had so much guilt keeping it from you. But you need to know; I told her to bury it and never bring it up. I knew the turmoil and strife it would create, so if you want someone to blame, blame me," he says.

"There's no one to blame. Mac didn't even remember Liv, which is astonishing but also reassuring. No lad wants another lad thinking about his lass, even if it was only once," Finn admits. "I need to prove to her that I want her in my life forever, so I need to make a statement. That's why I'm here. I want ye to help me pick out a ring."

"*An engagement ring?*" Garrett says in a surprised tone. "What's our budget?" he asks, quickly lightening the mood.

"What's yer cousin worth?" Finn jokes.

"I'll know it when I see it. When do you want to start looking?" he asks.

"I would love to surprise her with it in Indianapolis at the concert. Mellencamp was her and Dan's favorite. It's the one place that would mean the most to her, and I'd feel like Dan would be giving me his blessing." Finn says.

Finn and Garrett concoct a plan to get Red involved so they can pull off the big surprise.

#

"Operation Ring is underway," I say to Frank.

"I think it's so sweet that Finn wants to use the diamonds from my ring in Hank's, but there's no way Garrett will let that fly, nor should he. Their relationship is different and special. It deserves its own unique ring to symbolize their love."

"Garrett's version of defining the significance of their love is by the price tag, so hopefully he has deep pockets."

"She strikes me as the type who would be thrilled with anything," Frank says.

"You're right but Garrett's the one driving the transaction." I wink at her.

"Aww, it's stunning . . . " Frank says as we watch them settle on a single, 2.5 carat, oval diamond ring with a platinum band.

#

Finn puts the plan in motion with the girls and flies into Indianapolis to coordinate the big moment. First on the agenda is to visit Frank's parents to tell them about the engagement. He arrives and rents a car to have lunch with them in Seymour, Indiana. They haven't seen each other since the funeral, and he knows they still feel deeply connected to him. He dedicates the day to getting them caught up on the show, the new restaurant, and telling them about Hank.

"Part of the reason I'm here is because of someone I met who had a connection to Christine. Her name is Olivia Henry. I met her in California, and, well, we hit it off and began dating. Turns out she lost her best friend in a car accident not too long before Christine passed, which is how we initially bonded. Here's the insane part. Her best friend was Dan Sullivan."

Frank's mom gasps. "Oh my word, I just got goose bumps all over. I didn't know he had passed. That is just awful."

"I know, very tragic. Liv has had a very hard go of it. Ye know how Dan used to call Christine, Frank?"

"Yes," she says.

"Did Christine ever talk about Dan's friend from home named Hank?" he inquires.

"Yes, she said he called them his Hank and Frank," she replies.

"Well, Olivia Henry is Hank," he informs them.

"This is truly unbelievable," she says, attempting to process this information.

Finn fills them in on how they discovered the connection at his parents's anniversary party and how he and Liv are convinced that Christine and Dan are guiding them together. He shows them the photo album of the trip to Ireland.

"This is just incredible," Frank's mom says, going through each page in detail.

"This might sound like an odd question, but do you ever feel like Christine is around or trying to communicate with you?" Finn asks.

"Oh my goodness, all the time. We see rainbows, butterflies, pennies, feathers . . . you name it, and we've seen it."

"Liv is a big believer in signs and feels like Dan is always communicating with her. In fact, she's convinced he's with Christine on the other side." Her mom erupts into tears.

"Oh, I am so sorry, I didn't mean to . . ."

She puts her hand up to interrupt while trying to compose herself. "That . . ." she stutters, "brings me so much peace and comfort. What a gift. Thank you." She gives Finn a big hug. "So, how long are you in town?" she asks, attempting to change the subject to something more pleasant.

"That's another reason I wanted to stop by. I'm here for Olivia. She's meeting her girlfriends in Indianapolis for the John Mellencamp concert. I'm going to surprise her. I plan to propose."

"Oh Finn, that is such terrific news," she says, lighting up in excitement. "We are thrilled for you. Olivia sounds like a perfect match."

"Thank you, I think so, too. I wanted ye to hear the news from me."

"Well, you have our blessing, my dear," she states. "And I hate to break this up, but I'm hoping to get to the cemetery before it gets dark."

"Of course, of course."

She jumps up. "There is just one more thing . . ." she says as she disappears. When she returns, she hands Finn a letter. "Christine wrote this note about a month before she passed. She asked that I hold on to it and give it to you, but insisted I wait until you had enough time to heal. I never felt right about mailing it without giving you the explanation," she says. "So, now seems like the right time." She gives Finn a kiss on the cheek. "And again, we're just tickled pink about your news. It's so wonderful to see you, Finn. You stay in touch, okay?" she gushes.

"Thank you. I will." Finn clutches the letter on the way to the car.

#

Finn arrives to the cemetery just before dusk.

"He hasn't seen the grave with the headstone," Frank says.

That felt good. The timing was right. There was a reason to visit, and it all fell into place. They seem well. I know yer up there watching over them, but it sounds like they're keeping busy with yer nieces and nephews. They bring them a lot of joy, which is wonderful. Oh, and I got yer letter, but I'm going to wait until I see Mac and Jules in a few weeks before I open it. We're celebrating his thirtieth birthday, and I'm hoping maybe ye have a message for them, too. So, now on to the elephant in the room. You know why I'm here this weekend. You led me to Liv. I know you and Dan had a big hand in that, and for that I am forever grateful. I didn't think I would ever love again. I didn't know I would be capable of loving again after losing ye. I will always love ye. I don't want ye to think because I cleaned out the flat and gave the stuff to yer parents that I'm over it. I'll never be over it, but Liv brings happiness into my life again. She's a bright light. She's sweet and sexy . . . sorry . . . and funny. Ye found the perfect one for me if it can't be ye. I don't want to spend another day without her. Please watch over us and keep us safe, happy, and healthy. I love her and never want this feeling to go away. To be lucky enough to find it twice, in a lifetime, is a dream. My only request is I need to know that ye approve. That I have yer blessing. Tell Dan I'm sorry for being such a stubborn bastart and hurtin' Liv. I promise I'll take good care of her heart, forever.

"I wouldn't have it any other way, my love," Franks says as a butterfly lands on his leg.

I'll take that as a yes.

#

"She's going to flip," I say to Frank as the girls collect Hank from the airport and they drive over to the hotel. For the icing on the cake, "Small Town" starts playing in the car.

"You're joking. Are you playing this on your iPhone?" Hank says in disbelief.

"Nope. I swear. Look at the dashboard. It's playing on the radio," Red insists. "Danny is right here with us, just as it should be." She looks at Hank through the rearview mirror. She wells up with tears.

"Hellllooooooooooooo, I'm right here, per usual, " I say. Hank mustered up every ounce of energy she had to get here this weekend since she's still not spoken to Finn. These girls are the only reason she's here. They are her sisters in life. She would never miss an opportunity to see them. Plus, now they get to be with her to witness the best moment of her life. They settle in at the hotel then head to the venue where they're greeted by security and escorted inside. Her excitement starts to sink in.

I can't wait to meet Mellencamp and tell him all about Danny, and the special meaning and impact his songs have on my life.

"Here we go . . ." I say, grabbing Frank's hand. They're next up. The security guard approaches and has them follow him. He directs them to an unassuming door in the main hallway and radioes to gain permission to let them in.

"You go first, Liv. This is your night," Red says.

Hank presses down on the door handle. She's expecting to see John Mellencamp, but instead it's Finn dressed in a suit, surrounded by a sea of rose petals. She nearly collapses.

"This is so amazing. I wish I could go back and be a fly on the wall for so many of my special moments," Frank says.

Hank looks back at the girls with shock and awe, figuring out their roles in this scheme. They were all in on it. She's overcome with emotion as Finn reaches out to embrace her.

"Come here," he says, pulling her in tight, and the stream of tears begins to flow. He pulls her in to look into her eyes.

"Are you getting choked up, Danny?" Frank asks, rubbing my back.

"I'm so happy this moment is here for her. She's waited *so* long."

"God, I've missed ye, Liv," he says, kissing her. "I'm so sorry. Will ye forgive me?" he whispers into her ear.

"Finn . . ." she whimpers, unable to speak as he breaks away to get down on one knee. He reaches into his pocket, gasps come from the girls.

"Olivia Henry, I never want to spend another second away from ye. Will ye make me the happiest man in the world . . . will ye marry me?" he asks as tears fill his eyes.

She bursts into tears. "There isn't anything I want more . . . yes, yes, YES!" she responds as he stands up to put that flawless ring on her finger. "And I believe this is yer's, too," he says, holding up the necklace she thought she lost.

"Turn around and I'll put it back where it belongs." He reaches around to clasp it then places a kiss on Hank's neck.

"I thought I lost this . . . and you," she whimpers, grabbing his cheeks for a passionate kiss.

The girls give them space for a few minutes to celebrate before they can't resist joining in.

"The real question is, am I even going to meet John Mellencamp?" Hank jokes when she hears, "Well, I was born in a small town . . ." and he turns the corner. There isn't a dry eye in the room as he introduces himself. They exchange pleasantries, and Hank tells him my story n the short time she has. He is so gracious and touched by my story.

Danny, you overwhelm me. I love you so much. I can feel you right here with me. Thank you.

"I love you so much, Hank. I wouldn't miss this for the world . . . and this is just the beginning of the good news for you," I say.

#

This weekend is Mac's surprise birthday weekend in Tahoe.

"Tonight, we're celebrating some smashing news," Mac says as he raises his glass. Finn and Hank glance over at each other, expecting the next words out of his mouth to be Jules is pregnant. "I would like to congratulate the next famous screenplay writer . . . Olivia Henry."

Finn and Hank look at each other, perplexed.

"Liv, remember when you were on set and I asked ye if I could pitch yer manuscript around?" Mac asks.

"Yes," she responds.

"*The Man Guide* received an offer from the Beyond Dreams Production Company for a hundred and twenty-five thousand dollars yesterday," Mac announces.

"What he really means to say is Dan was a brilliant, handsome, hilarious charmer whose life is meant to be told on the big screen," I say to Frank.

"Bloody hell," Finn yells as he jumps up from his seat to kiss Hank. "This is brilliant. Absolutely brilliant."

Hank sits, stunned, trying to process what was just said. Tears stream down her cheeks as the shock settles in. "Are you kidding me? How? When?"

"My agent and I met with the production company yesterday about another project and I pitched it. This story has legs, Liv. You have a natural talent."

"See, Hank . . . you just need to trust me," I say.

"It's true. It's a gift," Finn chimes in. "Yer making a connection between the beyond and those who are still here. Everyone has lost someone they love. People want to have faith that their loved ones aren't truly gone. You've told it in a funny and relatable way that they will embrace."

"He's right, Liv. I think this is going to explode," Mac says.

"Never in a million years could I dream this . . . I wrote this on a whim, as an escape to a place where Dan and I could exist in the same world. Imagining he's guiding me to my destiny from the other side. It's almost as if I'm manifesting it."

"I'm so proud of ye . . . and so is Dan," Finn gushes as his eyes well up with tears of pride.

Danny, I know you have everything to do with this. I'd be skeptical if I didn't know for certain that people will fall in love with our friendship and this eternal connection. In my darkest moments since you've passed — the terrorist attack, Owen being sick, and Finn walking away from me temporarily, I dove into writing this love story. The love letter to you about our friendship. It's the only thing that has gotten me through. I escaped into a world where you are guiding, directing, and comforting me. A place where I have nothing but faith. I realize now the path you're leading me down is the journey back to myself. You aren't going to give me my happy ending until I learn to love myself again and put all my trust into the bigger and better plan. I'm getting in my own way with all my doubts and fears; I can see that clearly now. Thank you for your tremendous gift, for never giving up on me. I will love you forever and always.

"And now Finn is about to read them *the letters*. How blown away do you think they'll be when they figure out I actually told Finn to go find Hank?" Frank asks.

"To any *normal* human being, that would be a lifetime of proof that your Angel is manifesting things for you from the beyond. With Hank, it will last her until Tuesday before she loses all faith in me again," I say and Frank laughs. "Don't get me started," I say, rolling my eyes.

\#

ENTRY #10

My beloved Hank,

Congratulations! I never envisioned a day where I wouldn't be there to see all these big moments in your life. Getting engaged, you have a movie being made. You've blossomed into an amazing woman. I could NOT be prouder of you. You are phenomenal person, beautiful on the inside and out, and, most importantly, your undeniable spirit is back. The spark. The fire in your belly. Trust your instincts. Your confidence is shining through and I only have bigger and better things in store.

I love you forever and always,

Danny

CHAPTER FOURTEEN

The wedding weekend is here. Hank and Finn fell in love with the Texas Hill Country, so Tex offered to let them use his ranch for all the wedding festivities. Hank and Garrett went on a scouting trip and Garrett has done everything in his power to turn this into the most glamorous, rustic wedding a girl could ask for. It will be an intimate group of just under one hundred. Guests are staying at a bed and breakfast property nearby called Hayden Run Falls Inn.

Danny, this is it. It's finally here. I'm getting married. I'm so ready to marry this man. My heart is full. You know what I want from you as a wedding present? Send me something on our wedding day so I know you're there with us. Of course, I know you will be, but I want something big to feel your presence. Surprise me.

"Look at her," Franks gasps, seeing Hank in her dress. It's an elegant, muted white, A-line dress. It has wide straps merged into a low neckline covered with a sheer overlay, giving it an overall modest but classic look. The back is half-opened. The fitted bodice is embellished with an embroidered applique. The skirt drapes and falls away perfectly from her body.

"She is absolutely stunning," I say.

"Be still my heart, Danny. You've gotten even more sweet," Frank says.

"Seeing her with all her best friends and her dad about to walk her down the aisle, is just, well, overwhelming."

"It's breathtaking," Frank declares.

The ceremony is at dusk. The vow exchange will take place under a wicker arch, covered in flowers, overlooking the large pond. There are ten rows of long bench seating made from wooden tree stumps.

The reception is in the old barn on the property, with wide planked tobacco pine wood floors. It's broken up into quadrants to make it feel like multiple rooms. For dining, there are three long, handmade aged oak tables stretching across the floor to both ends for community dining. Each have formal table cloths. The casual chairs are spray painted in silver. Wild flowers in mason jars serve as centerpieces in front of every other place setting, along with dozens of lit candles. There is a gourmet buffet and bars at both ends of the barn with a dance floor. White linen fabric clothes are woven throughout the rafters and six giant crystal chandeliers with bulky chain link hang from the ceiling. In between are light bulb lights, dangling from exposed electric cords over the tables. The support beams are wrapped from ground to ceiling with white lights, creating ambience.

Old wine barrels hold large charcuterie boards full of meat, cheese, and other hors d'oeuvres. There are dozens of custom wine bottles with their initials and wedding date. Lanterns are strung from tree branches. A large fire pitis staged with big baskets of white, fluffy throws embroidered with the words *McDaniels Wedding* for guests to take home, surrounded by white Adirondack chairs, along with a s'mores bar, and tubs full of sparklers. Trees and potted plants are placed throughout the space, bringing the outdoors in and the walls are covered with faux curtains.

"Garrett didn't miss a detail. It's obvious how much he loves Hank. How lucky to have someone so special bring your fairy tale to life."

"Throw in the Chuck Taylors he's going to wear with his kilt to surprise her. Not one detail has been missed."

Danny, what do you think? Isn't it fabulous? Is this not going to be the best wedding a girl could ask for? The only thing that would make it perfect is having you there. Thank you from the bottom of my heart for helping me find Finn. I am so grateful. I'm finally overwhelmed with joy and happiness rather than darkness and despair. I will never accept that you won't be here with me, but I know you will be here in spirit and I love you. Forever.

#

"I thought I'd surprise you and make you dinner for a change. I figured you got used to not cooking while we were in Mexico," Hank says, handing Finn a glass of red wine.

"I could get used to this. What are you making? Smells delicious." He leans over to get a closer look.

"Pork tenderloin, asparagus, and garlic mashed potatoes."

"I'm impressed, Liv," he says.

"Go sit down while I finish." She pauses. "Oh wait, I forgot one thing . . . Frank, come here, boy."

Frank approaches, wagging his tail, an envelope in his mouth.

"Whaddya got there, bud?" Finn asks, bending down to retrieve the envelope from Frank. He opens it and reads it out loud. "Mommy says I'm going to be a big brother. Do you want a boy or a girl?" He looks at

Hank in disbelief. "A baby? Really, Liv?" he asks, welling up with tears. She nods in response and embraces him as he's collecting his thoughts, trying to absorb what he just heard.

"This is beyond brilliant . . . I'm going to be a da," Finn says.

"He'll be a great dad," I say to Frank.

"I love that his dream of being a dad is finally coming true," Frank adds.

"*Chuy* allowing us to meet and spend time with Dani, Hank and Finn's daughter, before Hank even found out she's pregnant, is mind blowing," I say.

"What about *HIM* blessing her with the gift of being able to see us? That's going to keep us connected on the deepest level," I say.

"Do you think they'll believe it?" Frank asks.

"Without a doubt. They're going to be phenomenal parents," I say.

#

Hank's baby shower starts today at four, so she starts her day at the cemetery to visit me in person. Since she's moved, she's better about not having to talk to me there but today is special. She wants me to see the baby up close.

Hi, Danny. How are you? It's been a while. I miss you. Am I ever going to get over the disbelief of you being gone forever? What would we be doing if you were still here? Would you be married? Would your wife be pregnant, too? Would our kids grow up together? Would we have drifted apart? Maybe we'd be so busy and wrapped up in our own lives that we'd only see each other at holidays and talk on our birthdays. I can't imagine that would be the case, but time is a luxury we take for granted. I have a constant reminder of how precious it is and how much every second should be treasured. Okay, enough sappy talk. Here is the baby. I think it's a girl, but everyone else is convinced it's a boy. I don't care. I want a happy, healthy baby. It's been such a wonderful experience feeling this human being moving and growing inside of me. Sometimes, I pretend you're giving me a swift kick when I need it. So, the real reason I'm here is because Finn and I have a very important question we want to ask of you and Christine, which is why I waited to come in person. We want you to be the baby's godparents. We know you're always watching over us, but we want you to love and protect this little one with everything you have. You are now guardian angels, so it's the only thing that feels right — for both of us. Just as she finishes, the sun darts out from behind a cloud like a glistening smile and a warm hug.

Perfect, I'll take that as an emphatic YES. We love you.

She gets in the car, turns on the ignition, and hears "Oh, oh, oh / Sweet child o' mine / Oh, oh, oh, oh / Sweet love of mine" playing by Guns N' Roses.

You never cease to amaze me, Danny.

"If she only knew what's in store," I say to Frank.

#

As the due date nears, Finn's growing more anxious. He's having flashbacks from the terrorist attack and is afraid something is going to happen with the baby. Hank makes him an appointment to see Kelly, the psychic medium, so he can ease some of his fears.

Christine, please help me get through this. Give me something concrete so I know you're here with me.

*Something undeniable and impossible for me to refute.
What I want most is to know that everything is going to be
okay with Liv and the baby. I cannot bear to go through
any more trauma. I don't know why I keep having these
nightmares. What are you trying to tell me? Please help me
understand what it is I'm sensing. I will always love you.
Tell Dan I say hi and thanks for the Mellencamp surprise.
Here goes nothing!*

"Hi, I'm Kelly, you must be Finn," she says,
extending her hand.

"Aye. Nice to meet ye, Kelly." He shakes her hand.

"Don't be nervous. I promise this won't hurt," she
says, laughing.

She gestures for me to follow her back to the room
where she'll be doing the reading. She gives him the
background on how she works and asks him to make
his three wishes.

1. *To keep Liv and our unborn baby healthy, safe,
   and fulfilled forever. I want Liv to realize her
   dreams and continue to inspire me by reaching for
   the stars.*

2. *For me to be the man of Liv's dreams, to continue
   to earn her love, respect, and trust, to never, ever
   take her or our love for granted, and to be the best
   da and provider to my children. Someone they are
   proud to call their husband and da.*

3. *My last wish is for Liv and me to live free from
   fear. To live a life knowing that God, through our
   own guardian angels, Dan and Christine, is
   protecting us and the ones we love, and will
   continue to give us strength and prosperity on our
   journey.*

"Okay, I'm ready," Finn says to Kelly.

"Let's get started." She closes her eyes and places her hands over his while whispering a prayer.

"Wow, right away I have someone here who is eager to get through. A young female in her early twenties. Do you know who this would be?"

"Aye," Finn says, catching his breath.

"She wants to say thank you for loving her and taking care of her. She knows how hard it was for you to let her go but she is at peace. There was nothing that could have been done. Any additional treatment would have prolonged the inevitable. You gave her permission to be free from pain."

"Brilliant." Finn wells up with tears.

"She's holding a little boy's hand and wants you to know they are together on the other side." He is almost paralyzed in disbelief.

Glorious, it was a baby boy.

"Incredible. We lost a baby, but we never knew if it was a boy or girl."

"She wants me to tell you how proud she is of you and all of your accomplishments. She's showing me a leaf . . . like an herb of some sort. Hmmm, this is weird. I've never seen this one before. It looks like something you would cook with? Like a green, leafy herb. Does that make sense?"

"Is it by chance, mint?"

"Yes! That's exactly what it is."

"After she passed, I was on a cooking reality show and won a head chef position at a restaurant in Vegas called Mint. That's amazing . . . wow."

"I'm hearing the name, Frank. Do you know who that would be?"

"Aye. That was her nickname in college and I have a golden retriever named Frank, after her." Finn smiles.

"Look at him," Frank says to me. "He's blown away. He had no idea I would be or could be so specific. There's no way Kelly could know any of this. She's hitting everything right on the head."

Before she ends their session, she asks him, "Is there anything else you want to know or want to ask?"

"Aye. Two things. The first — is she with anyone besides the little boy in heaven?"

"Let me check. Okay, yes, I'm hearing the name Danny. Do you know who that would be?"

"Aye, brilliant. That's exactly what I wanted to hear. My last question is related to my recent recurring dreams. Is everything going to be all right with Liv and the baby?"

"All she is saying is . . . trust me . . . over and over."

#

"Today is going to be a rough one," I say to Frank. Hank is in labor. They check into the hospital and she is settling into the idea that they are no longer a couple but leaving here as a family.

"I know. You can do this. She'll be waiting for you," Frank says as Hank's blood pressure drops, and she begins crashing on the table. She's rushed into the operating room for an emergency C-section. They won't let Finn in since it's turning into a life and death situation.

Dan and Christine, I'm imploring you . . . PLEASE help them. You can't take them from me. Neither of them. Why is this happening? Haven't we all been through enough? When will it be over? When can we start living?

Believing? Trusting? I just want to breathe again — live, love, and laugh without the fear of something bad happening. I know there are so many good things out there. We just need to find them. I am putting every ounce of my faith in you in this exact moment. Christine, you told me to trust you so that's what I'm going to do. I promise if they pull through, that we will name her in your honor. Whatever it takes. I will move past the old me and lead my life with passion and positivity. Liv is my soulmate. My best friend. My everything. I need her here with me . . . forever. Please, please help me. I need you to show me a sign that they will be okay.

Just as Finn finishes his prayer, his phone buzzes in his pocket. He pulls it out to find a text from Liv. All it says is *I love you.*

"DANNY!" she sobs, squeezing me as hard as she can.

"HANK, hi," I say, giving her a warm embrace. I had no idea how overwhelmed I would feel in this moment . . . getting to see her and talk to her. I am trying to savor the moment as this is the only time I get to see and speak to her.

"We don't have a lot of time," I say.

"What do you mean? Where am I?" she asks.

"You're at the gates of heaven but you're not supposed to be here yet."

"Why? What's happening?"

"Your heart stopped. You've lost a lot of blood, but the doctors will work hard to bring you back. You will be fine," I say as she gets emotional.

"But I don't know if I want to go back. I've missed you so much. I can't say goodbye again."

"Your baby girl needs you," I say.

"Baby girl? But we don't know what we're having."

We look down and see the doctors deliver the baby while they continue working to revive Hank.

"It's a beautiful, healthy baby girl. She needs you and Finn needs you . . . now more than ever."

"Thank you so much for finding him for me, Danny. I love him so much. I can't leave him. He wouldn't be able to take the sadness. He'd never recover. He misses Christine so much, too. Is she with you?"

"Finn was always planned as a part of your future. Even before you were born. There is always a plan. And yes, Christine is with me but wasn't allowed to come. We are together on the other side."

"What's it like? Heaven?"

"It's indescribable. Magical. Brilliant. Vibrant. The most glorious place you've ever seen."

"I love and miss you *so much* . . . you know that, right?"

"Yes, and me too, Hank. I'm always with you. In every moment. I will watch out for you and protect you from harm for all of eternity. It's my job on the other side. I'm a guardian angel to the ones I loved the most. The ones I left behind."

"Really? So, you can hear me when I talk to you and ask you for things?"

"Yes, but I'm only allowed to respond with signs and symbols. You're one of the lucky ones. You're in tune and learning how I communicate. You need to continue to trust and have faith. There are so many good things ahead for you and Finn. I promise. And I assure you, Christine and I will be the best godparents we can be to Danielle Christine."

"Oh, Danny, you can hear and see me." She hugs me, never wanting to let go.

"I know everything, even before you do. I am guiding you, Hank, but you must go. We must say goodbye for now. I will love you forever and always. We'll be together again someday, I promise."

"I love you, too, so, so, so very much."

"And Hank, God only has one rule, which allowed me to be here with you."

"What is it?"

"When you wake up, you won't remember our encounter. See you in your dreams." And with that, I must leave her. Frank and Jake are waiting for me at McGee's as I finish.

"That was harder than I thought it would be," I share.

"That's how I felt when I saw Finn during the terrorist attack. I wanted to pause the moment. I could live in the middle with him forever. I didn't want to let him go."

"I know but they have so much more life to live. It was a close call. The doctors had to perform a full hysterectomy to stop the bleeding," I say.

"Finn has been through this before but Hank will be just as devastated. Once they get to know Dani, short for Danielle Christine, they will realize they have all they would ever want or need. They named her after two special guardian angels."

"How sweet. She's a beauty. It will be hard for Hank to learn she can't have any more children, but this is another critical life lesson. Things may not happen in the way you dream or envision but *Chuy* always gives you what you need," Frank says.

#

Hank realizes the seriousness of the situation and is grappling with the news.

"But I want her to have a sibling," she bawls.

"I grew up without a sibling and I survived. I have Mac, he's my best lad. The brother I never had. She will have two adorable, doting cousins who will always watch out for her — Livey and Owen. I have something that might help cheer you up."

"What?" she asks.

"Close yer eyes," Finn instructs as he reaches into his pocket for her gift and places it in her hand. "Okay, open."

"What is it?" she asks, inspecting the jewelry.

"The lassies at the restaurant told me I had to get ye something called a 'push present.' It's a charm bracelet. I've been collecting charms in some of our favorite places. I know ye and Dan had that tradition, so I thought I would start one for us," he says as she starts to cry.

"Finn, this is so incredibly special. You're so thoughtful. How did I get lucky enough to find you?" she asks.

"The feeling is mutual, my dearest love." He kisses her as she investigates her new bling.

"Let me explain the different charms. This is an Eiffel Tower, where we first professed our love for each other; then we have a journal representing your future career as a famous writer; a spoon symbolizing me and the restaurant; a dog charm for Frank; wedding bells for our glorious nuptials; some maracas documenting our sexy honeymoon; a baby carriage for our sweet little Dani; and do you know what this last one is?" he asks as she takes a closer look.

"It looks like a couple of small buildings."

"No . . . it's a small town," he says, and she gasps in shock then starts to cry. This time they are happy tears.

"Oh, Finn McDaniels, you overwhelm me. I love you so much."

#

ENTRY #11

My beloved Hank,

I'm so happy your family is now complete. I knew Finn was the perfect man for you. He's charming, thoughtful, generous, passionate, giving, loving, and most importantly—he adores you and will continue to do so for the rest of the days of your life.

Chuy let me meet Dani before she was born into the physical world. She's going to be very special. She'll grow up and do incredible things.

I love you forever and always,

Danny

CHAPTER FIFTEEN

Hank is up early this morning to do Dani's feeding. Finn can hear her on the monitor.

"*Good morning, sweet pea. Did you sleep well? Huh? Let's get your diaper changed and we'll have some breakfast. How does that sound? Hmmm . . . Oh, oh, oh don't cry. It's coming, it's coming. I know, you're hungry. Here we go . . . there you are . . . that's what you wanted, isn't it? Sweet baby. God, I love you so much. How did we get lucky enough to be chosen as your parents? You know Daddy and I love you to infinity and beyond. But you know who else loves you? Your guardian angels. Their names are Danny and Christine. They are very, very special. They're your godparents, and their job is to always watch over you and protect you. They were Mommy and Daddy's best friends, but God needed them for some special work in heaven, so they aren't here with us anymore. Maybe you were with them before you came to us . . . maybe you already know them. They love you, too, very much. They were with us the day you were born, watching out to make sure we were okay. They will always love you, just as much as we do. See this mobile over your crib? This is what angels look like. They are white with beautiful wings. They are God's special helpers. Only the most special ones get to be with HIM.*"

\#

I meet Frank and Jake at McGee's for lunch. They have my tuna melt waiting for me when I sit down.

"Hank found out *The Man Guide* is green lit which means funding is secured and they have an official budget. The executive team is in the process of being selected: the casting director, cinematographer, and producers. Mac will be the Executive Director, which means he has full creative responsibility for making her story come to life on the big screen. They started scouting locations and they picked Austin, Texas, to do the filming. They are aiming for late spring next year. By then, Jane and her parents will be settled in Austin. Dani will be about nine months old," I catch Frank and Jake up to speed.

"That's crazy awesome. Isn't Hank's whole family about to move to Austin?" Jake asks.

"Yes. Jane's husband got transferred to Austin and her parents are about to relocate there, too. They want to retire, downsize, and be near the twins."

"And now Hank and Finn's lives are pulling them there, too. Now that Tex married a local woman in Palm Springs, ironically named Christine, Finn is going to hand over the reins of Christine's to him to manage the day to day. They win a Michelin star and Christine's takes off. They are going to expand their restaurant concept to Austin. Finn is anxious to put down roots close to Hank's family so Dani can grow up with cousins and grandparents," Frank explains.

"Hank has no idea but her whole life is leading her to Austin. First the wedding, now the movie. Garrett will soon be featured on a local home show which will lead him to opening a third store there, too. Jane will partner with him and start her own furniture line. You see, now that Hank is following her dreams, doors will begin to open for all of them." I say.

"Finn is looking in the area for new locations for the restaurant and stumbles on a large estate. He turns the home into a bed and breakfast and opens a new restaurant in the barn and builds a new home for them on the property," Frank adds.

"Their happily ever after?" Jake asks.

#

"Finn made all the arrangements to get Red, Liza, and Alexa here for the movie premiere. Hank has no idea. She thinks she and Finn get to attend the premiere as Mac and Jules' guests. The plan is to have everyone waiting inside after she walks the red carpet," I say as we see her standing in a spaghetti strap, pale pink, full-length gown with a sweetheart neckline, sequins covering the bodice. Her hair is pulled up and back off her face, and her makeup is soft but stunning.

"Has it sunk in yet that we're driving over to yer movie premiere?" Finn asks.

"Pinch me just in case," she jokes.

"I'd like to make a toast to my stunning, talented, and entertaining wife whom I love beyond measure. I know what it took ye to get here to this moment. Yer resilience, tenacity, and resolve is nothing short of astonishing. Ye inspire me every single day. Dani is blessed to have such a strong, generous, and confident mum to look up to. I'm so proud of ye, Liv. Cheers to ye." He raises his glass.

"Cheers, my love. Right back at you. We're turning into quite the little power couple," she quips. The limo pulls up and she sees the theater. "Aw. The theater reminds me of the place back home I went to with Danny when we got kicked out."

The surprise is off to a great start. They stand in line to get their picture taken in front of the sponsor screen. As Hank makes her way inside, she sees everyone in the crowd and begins to cry. "Did you do this?" she says.

"Aye. Surprise," I whisper.

"Finn McDaniels, thank you. I love you so much," she says as Red, Alexa, and Liza smother her in hugs and kisses. She's thrilled to have them here to celebrate this monumental night. Just before they sit down, Red pulls Hank aside and hands her an old yearbook. She opens the yearbook, takes a deep breath, trying to hold back her tears, and reads it.

> *My beloved Hank,*
>
> *Where do I start? Here we are at the end of the road with endless possibilities ahead. I wish I could say I was nothing but excited but if I'm being honest, I'm more apprehensive and anxious. The unknown can be a scary place, especially when you know what you're leaving behind. I can say, without a doubt, that these last four years in high school were the best of my life.*
>
> *The reason for that is largely due to you and our forever friendship. I know we're going to be physically separated now but you will always be in my heart. Nothing can ever break our unique and special bond. You are one of a kind and I'll never be lucky enough to meet another girl like you. Although we never had a romantic connection, I do believe you are one of my soulmates and we'll*

always be deeply connected. We don't need to see each other to understand how special this is. We will know in our souls. I wish you the best on the amazing journey ahead. No matter where I am, I will always be your biggest cheerleader. Now go kick some ass!

I love you forever,

Daniel

"Aww, she's never read this before?" Frank asks.

"No, Red had the yearbook all of these years so she never read it before tonight."

"Wow, what an unforgettable moment," Jake says.

"This is nothing. Watch Finn surprise her with their new home and restaurant . . . " I say.

#

They pick up Dani and the limo escorts them to the property. Finn has Hank blind-folded until they arrive for the unveiling.

"Liv, this isn't just the new restaurant. This is our new B&B. It's going to be a family business. Your parents, Jane, Peter, Garrett, and Tristan have all agreed to help run this place. We wanted to have a legacy in the family, something to leave for Dani and the twins someday," he says and begins to take her on a tour. "Here is the restaurant where we'll serve breakfast to our guests every morning," he says, showing her the French doors stenciled with the logo, *Dani's Café.* Hank has no words. Tears stream down her cheeks when Finn embraces her.

"You better buckle up because we're just getting started." He kisses her forehead. They finish walking the grounds and head toward the barn.

"Are you ready?" he asks, gesturing for her to close her eyes as he guides her to the side of the barn.

"I'm not sure. I'm already so blown away. How could you possibly have more?" she asks.

Attached to the side of the barn is a giant sign that reads *Hank's BBQ Heaven*.

"Are you kidding me?" she sobs as they swing through the kitchen and end up in the office where he has yet another surprise. He has black and white poster-sized photos of Christine and I hanging on the wall.

"*Wait for it . . .* " I say to Frank and Jake.

Dani shouts and points at the posters on the wall. She lights up and becomes animated.

"Finn. . ." Hank steps closer to the poster and prompts Dani. "Who is this?" she says, pointing at the poster of Dan.

"Baba," Dani yells without hesitation. She has a giant grin on her face and begins to gesture in sign language for more.

"They realize Dani can actually see us," I reveal, waving at Dani to get her attention. "They get it now. The toys moving around that they couldn't explain — the smiling, giggling, and babbling at things they couldn't see. Wondering how she learned sign language, her obsession with Hank's charm bracelet? They believe," I say.

"We always knew you were special," Finn says.

"She's been trying to tell us all along, haven't you, sweet baby?" Hank says.

"I never told you this, Finn, but when we couldn't explain things, I asked Danny for a sign. I told him he had to prove to me, so I knew I wasn't crazy. I said it had to be bullet proof so there would be absolutely no doubt. The sign would have to be crystal clear and here it is. Wow," Hank says. "I know we sense and feel them around but Dani can *see* them. This is our secret forever. The three musketeers."

CHAPTER SIXTEEN

Hank wakes up and takes a walk out to the big oak tree on the property while Dani and Finn are still sleeping. She's reflecting on the journey over the last several years. She approaches the tree and carves in a heart with the words *Dan + Liv.*

Danny, this heart symbolizes our forever bond. You're etched into my heart for eternity. I know this is all your doing — Finn, Dani, the writing, the movie, our new life and home. I know you made a special pact with the big guy in heaven. Please tell HIM thank you. You continue to be the very best friend any girl could hope or dream for. I know you know how much I love and miss you. I would give anything to have you back, but if I can't, this is the next best thing. I get to carry you around with me, always, in my soul.

Despite all the doubts, the tears, the one-sided fights and tantrums, I know you're here . . . always. I know that life is not going to be easy, but you've given me back the faith, hope and love I need to endure each and every storm. For that, I am forever grateful. I could have never imagined a dream this good. This is your way of proving to me we made it together. I'm honored and proud to be the one to share you with the world. You're even better than I remember. I love you, forever and ever, with all my heart.

#

Chuy is waiting for me when I arrive at *HIS* office.

"Well?" *HE* asks.

"Well . . . I'm humbled and beg for Your forgiveness for ever doubting You. This has been a long, hard, sometimes exhausting journey but she did it. She made it. She believes — without a doubt."

"Do you know why, Daniel?" *Chuy* asks. "Because you never, ever gave up on her."

Tears well up in my eyes. "I could never give up on her."

"I'm proud of you, Daniel. You've fulfilled your role. Hank knows now that you will always be with her — helping her, guiding her, and she'll no longer doubt your love or presence."

And with that *HE* concludes our meeting. As I leave, I begin to reflect on all the moments and lessons. I realize the bigger message and know I'm ready for whatever comes next.

#

ENTRY #12

My beloved Hank,

WE DID IT!!!!!! It's taken a ton of convincing, patience, and persistence but I know, without a doubt, that you believe that I'm here and never going anywhere. I promise to always guide and protect you and keep you from harm. You'll have weak moments, where you'll waver, but you can't ever deny our unspeakable bond. Nothing can penetrate what we have.

Now, it's time for me to go find MY soulmate . . .

I love you forever and always,

Danny

#

I see Jake just ahead of me walking towards McGee's. His cousin is meeting him today. She died of pancreatic cancer a year before he got here. I've been anxious to meet her. She sounds like she's just my type. "Wait up," I call out. "I want you to introduce me to your beautiful cousin, Jenny."

THE *Beyond* SERIES

Book 1: Beyond Believing

Book 2: Beyond Love

Book 3: Beyond Forever

Book 4: The Dan Diaries

d.d. loves to connect with her audience!
Sign up for her newsletter here:

www.ddmarx.com

CPSIA information can be obtained
at www.ICGtesting.com
Printed in the USA
LVOW13s0527050418
572329LV00007B/18/P

Dan Sullivan was the best friend o[...] [...]
taken in a tragic car accident. Sh[...] [...]
Dan navigates his way by learning [...]
first assignment is as Olivia's guardian angel. He has the crucial
role of guiding her to her pre-defined destiny. Dan's death throws
Olivia into a tail spin which causes her to veer way off course. He
understands the enormity of the challenge when he hears the
mechanism by which he can communicate. He's only allowed to
use signs and symbols to get her attention and cannot interfere
with her free-will.

Every time he thinks he's close, something throws her off track. He's
forced to start over by convincing her to trust in their enduring,
unbreakable bond. Olivia can feel Dan's presence but is still reluctant
to believe the messages he's sending. She is fearful of falling in love
again at the risk of losing another soulmate. Can Dan persuade her
to trust in his love from afar so she can finally receive the happiness
she truly deserves?

"The Dan Diaries demonstrates just how powerful the eternal connection can be
when you leave your heart open to receive messages from your loved ones. D.D.
Marx demonstrates this in such a true and beautiful fashion in her new book."
~ Kelle Sutliff, Psychic Medium and Author of 'Listen UP! The Other Side IS Talking'

D.D. Marx is a contemporary romantic fiction
writer and blogger, as well as a lover of all
things social. She is a graduate of the University
of Dayton, as well as the Second City program
in Chicago, where she currently resides. A
proud aunt and self-described hopeless
romantic, Marx has always had a knack for
humorous and engaging storytelling. Her pen
name is a dedication to her beloved friend
Dan, who continues to guide and inspire her
in her daily life.

US $10.95
ISBN 978-0-9972481-7-3
51095
9 780997 248173

FICTION / Romance